THE DADDY DILEMMA

A HOT SINGLE DAD ROMANCE #3

ANGEL DEVLIN

TRACY LORRAINE

A NOTE

Single Daddy Seduction is written in British English and contains British spelling and grammar. This may appear incorrect to some readers when compared to US English books.

Two years ago

"BRANDON. You have huge sweat patches under your arms for fuck's sake. Couldn't you have cleaned up your act just for once? It's my brother's engagement party."

My best friend's sister, Reese, stands with her hands on her hips, head tilted, as she looks over me with disdain. She's always acted like a brat on the few occasions I've seen her before, but since she passed the bar and became a hotshot lawyer, she really seems to think she's something. She's something all right. An Ice Queen bitch.

I give her what I hope is a withering look in return. "I'm well aware of that, Reese. I'm just hot. Something you'd probably not know about due to the vast layers of ice constructed around yourself." I'm usually a nice guy but I don't like being judged by someone who doesn't even know me.

"Hot is definitely not a word I imagine is usually associated with you. I don't know how my brother manages to be near you without vomiting. You're a slob."

"You're a bitch. I can clean up, but can you thaw, Ice Queen?" I shout back.

"Fuck you," she says and stomps off. I'm not pleased at how I've just acted, but who is she to come over and pass judgement on me? She doesn't know me. I've met her less than a handful of times. I get another beer from the bar and look around me. I watch Reese. She stops and talks to people but the smile she puts on her face never reaches her eyes and she keeps tidying up, taking empty glasses and plates over to the bar. What the fuck is she playing at? She sees me watching and slides two fingers up her cheek at me. Such a child. I walk over to the buffet table and pick up a sausage roll and then I eat it without a plate, watching the pastry flakes hit the floor with satisfaction. I can feel the burn of her stare and sure enough when I look at her, her gaze is zeroed in on me. If her eyes narrowed any more they'd just look like lines on her face.

I sigh. This is a fucking drag and I'm bored. I can't believe my best mate is any happier. The stupid things people do for love, like holding engagement parties in function rooms above noisy pubs. No thanks. And then their best mates have to come way, way, waaayyy out of their comfort zones to attend, and have to basically stand by themselves because they don't know many people and the ones they do know are busy. Case in point, Jack's parents had a messy divorce and both are present, slinging bitter looks at each other from across the room. It makes me wonder how Jack isn't put off marriage for life, but as I watch him and his bride-to-be beaming at each other, I can see the true love pass between them both.

I'm so happy for him but God, no thanks. I've had my heart broken once. Smashed to smithereens by a woman I'd thought was my everything. Now my heart is padlocked firmly shut, and I only have to see women like Reese to confirm that I'm better off alone. I pity the poor bloke who ends up with her. She'd be better off marrying a vacuum cleaner, because only some sucker would go there.

God, it's hot in here. I can feel my underarms getting wetter. I run a hand through my mid-length wavy hair. Yep, it's wet through at the back. Reese is right. I am a slob. But she doesn't know me, doesn't know why I am like I am, and she has no fucking right to stand there and judge me, like I'm on trial for crimes against barbers.

I stay another thirty minutes and then I say my goodbyes to Jack and his fiancée Rhian. I'm just at the door when she appears again.

"For someone who can't imagine why people want to be near me, you don't seem to be able to keep away," I snap.

"I just want the satisfaction of shutting the door on you. You really ought to do something with your appearance."

"And you really need to do something with your personality."

"Bye, slob."

"Sit on one of your own icicles, Ice Queen."

I walk out without looking back and hope it's a long time before I have to see Reese Connors again.

BRANDON

December

"THIS IS AN INTERVENTION, MATE."

The voice of my best mate, Jack, booms from about a foot away from me. Am I still asleep? Is this a dream Jack or a real Jack?

I realise it's a real Jack as I roll onto my back, a corner of something digging in my thigh painfully as I do so. Rubbing at my eyes, I sit up and squint. The bastard's opened the curtains and winter sunshine lasers through my vision. I bet I have empty sockets now. Eyeballs disintegrated. What the fuck is digging in my leg? I reach down and unearth a pizza box from underneath me. I'm still wearing my uniform from LoCost, the bargain warehouse I work nights at as a manager. I feel hot and sweaty despite it being winter. Oh, that might be because I turned the thermostat up on my way in last night. I don't think I'll want to open my heating bill.

"You awake yet?"

I nod though I'm not sure it's the truth. I watch as Aiden, my ex-housemate walks into the room. Ah, now I see how Jack got in.

"Wassgoinnonn?" I mumble.

"What's going on, my friend, is that we're taking you in hand. Enough is enough. You've been slobbing around for long enough and since Aiden left you've got a whole lot worse. I get married in a week's time. A week. You will not spoil my bride's Christmas Eve wedding by turning up looking like a hobo. We're Queer Eye-ing you.

That wakes me up. What the hell is that?

I stare at him wide-eyed. "What does that mean? It sounds sexual. Anything weird should be happening to you at your stag do." I startle as a thought comes to me. "Oh shit, is that tonight?"

"Yes, it's tonight. It's in... let me see." Jack looks at his watch. "Five hours time. Five hours to do something with you. Now Queer Eye, you muppet, is a Netflix show where five gay guys make people over. Clothes, hair, cooking skills, house, and life."

Now I'm starting to feel very worried about where this is headed. I think my head is where it's headed.

Aiden pipes up. "You're needing someone to share with to pay half the rent when my notice period is paid up. I paid you until the end of January because moving out at Christmas sucks, I know, but you need to get yourself and this house in order." He looks around the place taking in discarded beer cans, takeaway cartons, and is that an actual pair of my briefs? "No one is going to move in *here*." He says the word like most people say the word Brexit, i.e. with high disdain and as if it's the worst subject in the whole world.

He hands me a coffee, one I thought he'd made for himself. Mmmm, he's made it just as I like it. I miss Aiden making me coffee and it's only been a couple of weeks since he moved out. He fell in love. Can't blame him. Kaylie is lovely. I knew he wanted her before he did, the idiot. "How's Kaylie?" I ask, taking a sip of the hot beverage.

"We're not here to talk about Kaylie. We are here for you and the clock is ticking. Get that down your neck, go get the quickest shower in history, and then we're off to the centre of London, my friend, where you are booked to have your hair restyled, and we doing some clothes shopping. Oh and I saw your bank statement, so I know you've been saving your earnings since the end of time and have more than enough for some new threads. We're buying you a whole new wardrobe including clothes for tonight. And I've also organised someone to come around later in the week to help you sort through this mess of a house. When New Year is out of the way, you get this place advertised, you hear? And you keep it tidy. We'll be watching you."

Aiden points two fingers at his eyes, then at me and then back at himself.

My mouth has fallen open. In all the time I house-shared with Aiden he moaned at me plenty, but then usually had a mad tidy up himself and just threw my shit in my room. But now he seems so... fierce.

"But I like my hair," I protest, holding onto my shoulder-length locks.

"Nope. Goodbye to lanky locks, goodbye to the bird's nest you have going on around your chin." Jack has his hands folded across his chest in a 'brook no argument' stance. "Do what you like after the wedding, but you're looking shipshape for my big day."

"I fully intended to shower for it."

"Nope, Reese is right. You need a tidy up."

My shoulders tighten. I might have known she'd be behind all this. I've not seen her since the engagement party. I'll tolerate her at the wedding and then at the reception I'll make sure I'm at the opposite end of the room. If she comes over passing judgement on me, I might just be tempted to stick the bride's bouquet where the sun doesn't shine. God, what is it about her? I'm the most easy-going person I know but she brings out my inner twat.

My drink is taken out of my hand and I'm dragged off the sofa and pushed in the direction of the shower. My God, what is actually happening in my life right now? And do I have any clean towels?

I'M SITTING in a chair at the barbers while some bloke oohs and aahs while he runs his hands through my hair twisting it this way and that. Then his hands lift up. "Okay, I know what I'm doing here. We totally have a bit of a Jackson from Grey's

Anatomy going on under all this hair. I'm going to unearth him and you can thank me by giving me a huge tip. And if you don't swing that way then money is also good." He winks. My so-called friends are in hysterics.

I don't remember the last time I had short hair. I feel exposed and he's not cut a single hair on my head yet. I'm only doing this for my best mate. Once his wedding is over, I can grow it all out again.

The clippers come out and half an hour later I'm unrecognisable. My light brown hair is short and shaved at the sides. My beard is shaved so I now just have a dark scruff around my chin and above my lip. It's all so... neat.

I don't realise I've said this out loud.

"Exactly. That's what we're going for and what you need in all aspects of your life," Jack says, sounding like he's parroting what I imagine his sister said to him. "Neat and tidy. Now I'm booking you back in here the day before the wedding to make sure you're still looking this way. But for now, let's go get you some new clothes."

I follow them into a department store, where, to my embarrassment, they have booked a personal shopper to assist me. I'm given no say in the matter as a small fortune is hung on a side rail for me to purchase. Shirts, suits, shoes, new underwear, socks. You name it, it's here. Then they take me for a manicure and pedicure. I'm. Going. To. Die. And now thanks to my lack of hair, my bright red cheeks are free for the beauticians to see.

"Don't be embarrassed, honey. We have men in here all the time. Manscaping is so in fashion right now."

If they've booked me in for a back, sack, and crack, I am out of here. I have limits. Aiden and Jack block the exit, smug smiles playing on their lips. They have, the bastards.

I'm deposited back at my house after a much-needed couple of beers. I couldn't face lunch. I lost my appetite around the same time I lost my arse hair. I feel like one of those cats with no fur.

"Get some of those clothes on and we'll see you at XCluSiv in an hour," my ex-friends shout as they depart. "Oh and the cleaning service I booked work with hoarders, so don't stress," adds Aiden.

The door bangs shut behind them and I take a seat at my kitchen table feeling utterly violated and vulnerable.

After ten minutes of trying to process what just happened to me, I realise I'm down to fifty minutes to get ready, so I pick up some of the many bags and take them to my bedroom. I strip naked and stand in front of my bathroom mirror. A person I used to know stares back at me, though he's a lot older than the one I remember. This man hasn't been here for years, slowly let go as it became easier to escape from real life as much as possible. I'm glad they left me with the stubble as that's the only thing along with a few fine lines that sets me apart from the man who dated Naomi, the man made to feel so insignificant he disappeared. I re-affirm my vow in front of the mirror that no woman will ever do that to me again.

Maybe I have let myself go completely and maybe it really is time to try to do something. Aiden is telling the truth when he says I need to change my ways for a new housemate. I'll dip a freshly pedicured toe in the water tonight and see how it goes.

I put on the sharp grey suit trousers along with a pale white shirt shot through with a delicate grey stripe, and a black and grey tie. Shiny shoes. Brand new aftershave.

I'm a brand-new Brandon.

I call for a cab and I'm on my way.

We drink and move on, drink and move on.

We're all hammered. We've dressed Jack in a pink tutu over his trousers and put him a 'bride to be' sash on. The women out tonight all seem full of questions. It's been ridiculous. "Can you point me in the direction of the bar?" "Where did you get that gorgeous tie?" And they're all touchy-feely: a hand at my back or on my chest while they fondle my tie. It's just a bit of cloth for fuck's sake.

I complain to Aiden. "What is wrong with these women?"

"What are you talking about?" he asks and I explain.

He places a hand over his face.

"Fucking hell, Brandon. How long have you been out of the game, mate? They're hitting on you. They don't give a shit where you got your tie from. They just want it binding their hands together as you fuck them from behind."

I suddenly feel amazingly sober.

They are. They're hitting on me. I'm so far out of practice I haven't even realised.

***

MONDAY COMES AROUND and so does this organiser woman, Janet. She looks to be about forty and she sits with me at my kitchen table having taken a tour of the house. I'll need to go to work soon so I'm hoping she's not going to get too cosy here.

"There's a lot of clutter here, Brandon, and to me it seems like there's an underlying theme of avoidant behaviour. Like you're not facing up to things. Just like the barber revealed your face, it's time for us to work through the house and reveal the new Brandon here too. Someone who drops their laundry in a basket and if he can't switch a washing machine on regularly, uses a laundry and ironing service. We're going to find the real Brandon amongst all this chaos. Okay?"

I nod, ignoring all this psychobabble she's coming out with. If I keep the house clean for a few weeks I can get a new housemate. That's all I'm bothered about.

It's a difficult week because every afternoon before work Janet is there asking me what clutter is for recycling, the bin, or to stay. But slowly the house is revealed and she has me invest in some new furniture and bedding for my room and even calls in a decorator.

JACK COMES to stay at mine the night before his wedding as he and Rhian live together and she's getting ready at their place.

We have a couple of beers.

"I'm thinking I might regret getting you made over. You might outshine me on my big day." He laughs.

"Soon as this wedding is over, I'm just going to grow it all right back, you know that right?" I tell him.

He squeezes the top of my arm. "No. Please don't do that, Brandon. You look good, more than good, and the place looks great. It's hard. Change is hard. I know that. But it really is time for this brand-new Brandon. Same fab personality, but, well, clean."

"Thanks."

He grins. "That's what best mates are for."

He holds up his beer.

"To our new futures. To my bride and to brand-new Brandon."

We chink glasses.

Maybe I could give this new way a try?

2

REESE

"REESE, IT'S CHRISTMAS FOR GOODNESS' sake. Please go home."

I turn around and look at my boss, Clive.

"You're still here," I retort.

"Yes, because I'm waiting for you to leave before I can lock up the premises." He sighs.

"Oh. Sorry. I just had a few things to finish up."

"You know I admire your work ethic, Reese, but isn't your brother getting married?"

I nod. "Don't remind me. If Christmas isn't boring enough, I have to suffer a family wedding. Why they couldn't elope I don't know."

Clive rests against the door. "And that's why I love my favourite lawyer. Hard as nails. But suffer through it you have to, just like I have to go home and suffer through my in-laws." He looks down the corridor. "Right, I'm just going to evict Rich now, and then I might finally be able to lock up."

I pass Rich on my way down to the parking garage under the office block. "I had a party I could have gone to this afternoon," he bitches.

"So why didn't you?" I shrug.

"And let you look like the better employee? No fucking way. That upcoming partnership is mine."

I shrug again. "May the best lawyer win."

"Glad you feel that way. Why don't you just quit, get a husband, and make babies; like you females are supposed to do? Leave us blokes to run the world."

I come up to my car, my brand-new Mazda MX-5 RF, in its sleek, shiny grey. "Have a great Christmas, Rich, because your New Year isn't going to be so good when I get that partnership and all you'll probably get is crabs."

I leave him standing there like the dickhead he is as I screech out of the car park.

Men like him are the reason I stay single. The ones who feel a woman's worth is measured by how good at cooking and blow jobs they are. Don't get me wrong, there are cold nights when I wonder what it might be like to have someone there to cuddle me and let me warm my feet on them, but I only have to be at work the next day for that idea to fade away.

Better to stay an Ice Queen as Brandon fucking Weston calls me. God, I have to put up with him over Christmas. After the wedding where I have to stand near him, I'll keep to the other side of the room. Although I'll make sure to snigger over the fact he's had to have a haircut for the wedding thanks to my suggestion via Rhian that was she sure Brandon wouldn't ruin the wedding photos she had to keep for life.

Ha.

To be honest, all I wanted was for him to make an effort for my brother, my best person in the whole world. The boy and man who looked out for me when our parents were at war. I just felt it was the least Brandon could do. When I saw him at the engagement party it raised my hackles that he didn't respect my brother enough to tidy himself up.

Stop giving brain space to Brandon Weston. I chastise myself.

ONCE HOME I reluctantly start packing. Finally, I place my last item in my overnight bag and then check it off on my list before mentally running through everything I'm going to need for the short stay away for my brother and best friend's wedding and Christmas.

I love my brother. I love my best friend. I hate weddings, or any place where my parents have to be in the same room. I'm not surprised that Rhian is taking the plunge before me, although I often question her sanity for picking my big brother to tie the knot with.

My beautiful and quiet apartment is my haven and I'm loathe to leave it. However, convinced that I'm sorted, I zip my bag closed and lift it from the edge of my bed, ensuring that I smooth the bedsheets out.

Closing the door firmly behind me, I make my way through my apartment. I gaze out at the River Thames in the distance and wonder what the next few days have in store for me. At least Rhian took my suggestion for the wedding cake and ordered a huge tower of cupcakes instead. My mouth waters at the thought alone.

I swore off the idea of marriage the day I watched my parents attempt to divide everything up including my brother and me. That whole experience put me off the idea of relationships full stop, if I'm being honest. It also determined my future career path. I finished school and got into one of the best law courses in the country to prepare myself for becoming a family lawyer. I was determined that where I could, I'd try to make the whole process easier, for the kids if not the parents.

Focus. Determination. Precision. Those are the words I live by. There's no time in my life for the fakery of hearts and fucking flowers that turns to broken hearts and withered stems. I save all the heartbreak for work.

My eyes glance around my home, making sure everything is in order, before I shrug on my coat, scarf, and gloves and head out of my West Bank apartment.

The traffic is beyond a joke and by the time I pull up outside Rhian and Jack's building, my road rage is beginning to get the better of me. It's not helped by the fact that the only space I can find is just a couple of inches too small to allow me to parallel park my car with any ease.

"Fucking London," I mutter as I pull back and forth a few inches in an attempt to straighten up.

This is exactly why I bought a place with a designated parking space.

I'm a hot mess by the time I haul my bags up to their fourth-floor apartment.

Knocking, I smooth my hair down and run my fingers under my eyes to collect any straying make-up.

"Evenin', lil' sis." Jack raises a blonde brow. "You're looking... stressed. My girl getting to you?"

"No, she's a walk in the park," I lie.

In all honesty, Rhian hasn't been that bad with her wedding plans. What I struggle with the most is our polar-opposite styles. Where I go for minimalist everything, she's all about the lovey-dovey cute shit.

Her wedding theme is obviously Christmas, but instead of the traditional red or green, she went for a neutral pastel colour theme with sparkle and glitter everywhere. The whole thing hurts my head and it's pained me to help her plan it. Don't even get me started on the dress she's chosen for me. I'm so far out of my comfort zone I need planning permission.

He moves to the side of the doorway and gestures. "Come in, she's waiting for you."

"Why are you even here anyway?" I query.

"We shouldn't be seeing your ugly face tonight, so hop it."

"Yeah, yeah. I'm going, don't fuss. Brandon's waiting for me."

My eye-roll is so strong it actually hurts to the point I think I have given myself a small eye strain. "I can't believe you're staying at his place tonight. You sure you won't get eaten alive by whatever's living in his flat?"

"It's been tidied up. So has he. You won't recognise him tomorrow."

"If you say so." Dropping my bags at his feet, hoping he'll carry them the rest of the way, I slip past him in favour of my best friend.

"Reeeeese!" she squeals, running towards me from her position at the kitchen sink. She quickly flicks the bubbles from her hands and comes running over to throw her arms around me. "Can you believe I'm getting married tomorrow?"

"No, I really can't. Especially not to him." I screw up my face in disgust at the thought. "At least I'm gaining an awesome sister-in-law."

"You know you love me," Jack shouts.

I grin back at him. "It's the only reason I'm here because I love you both! Weddings, ugh."

"Stop it. My wedding's going to be awesome."

Rhian slaps my arm. "Are you going to tell me what we're doing tonight yet?"

"Nope, it's a surprise. But what I can tell you is that it does not involve washing up or your soon-to-be husband. He needs to leave." I say the last bit loudly to ensure he hears.

"I'm going. Pain in the arse," he mutters from somewhere in the flat.

I find a half decent bottle of wine in Rhian's fridge and pour myself a glass while the two lovebirds say their emotional goodbyes.

"You two are aware that you'll see each other tomorrow to commit your lives to each other, right?" I call when I hear Rhian sniffling in the hallway.

"It'll happen to you, you know?" Jack raises his middle finger and then blows me a kiss.

"Don't put a bet on that, you'll lose." I leave them to their final farewell.

I've almost drained my glass by the time Rhian joins me.

"So, can you tell me what we're doing now?" She sits on the sofa fidgeting with excitement.

"You'll find out in ten minutes. In the meantime, drink a glass of this and go and change."

I hand over a bag and she eagerly dives inside.

"Oh my god. I can't believe I get to wear this," she squeals excitedly, pulling out a vest and robe that have 'Bride' emblazoned on the front in pink glitter. "Thank you." She throws her arms around me before running from the room to change.

She bounces back into the room. "You got stuff for yourself, right?"

Everything inside me screamed that it was wrong when I placed the order online, but Rhian's my best friend and soon to be sister-in-law and if she wants the whole wedding experience then she'll damn well get it. Pulling out my own bag, she squeals louder and forces me to go and get dressed.

I'd organised for a couple of beauty therapists to come and give us both the whole works tonight. When I suggested going out, Rhian shot me down saying she wanted a relaxed night in before the crazy started tomorrow, so that's exactly what she's got.

"Oh and here. I bought you some bridal style cupcakes. Look, they're vanilla with icing confetti on."

Rhian shakes her head. "Oh they're for me are they? Not for the cupcake addict amongst us?"

"I couldn't resist." I giggle as I pick one up and start nibbling at the icing.

So we're pampered and preened, and then we have another glass of champagne while Rhian chatters excitedly about becoming Mrs Connors tomorrow. I say another silent prayer that the marriage of my brother and best friend works out because the fallout would be a heartbreak I'm not sure I'd survive, never mind them.

***

WHEN I AWAKE to the sounds of her starting the coffee machine first thing the next morning, I'm surprised to find I actually feel relaxed and almost ready for what lies ahead. It's hard not to get caught up in Rhian's excitement. She's absolutely buzzing. I love her dearly; she's family to me whether or not she's my brother's intended.

I've barely had my first coffee when the buzzer goes off and Rhian's mum, sister, and her two small nieces come barrelling in to get ready with us.

The morning is utter chaos but seeing the wide smile on my best friend's face makes it all worth it.

Before I know it, I'm donning my cream chiffon, layered, and embroidered lace dress ready to climb into the limo to head towards the church.

"Aw, Reese," Rhian cries when I step into her

living room. "You look gorgeous." Her eyes get a little wet as she stares at me.

Rhian and I met at university. She was also studying law although she's not really used much she learnt during her degree, preferring instead to work in a jewellery store. I've tried to convince her more than once to put everything she learnt to good use, but she always point blank refuses, explaining once again how becoming a lawyer was her parents dream, not hers, and how she loves seeing her customers faces light up when they choose the perfect piece of jewellery. She's a born romantic. I like to think she softens my edges and I remind her of the reality in her dreaming.

"Now, come on. No crying. That make-up artist spent way too long on it for you to ruin it before you've even left the house. Babe, it's your turn. Go and get in that dress. Here comes the bride."

She squeals again. Her clenched fists shake in excitement like a little girl and she runs for her room.

She stops and turns outside the door. "Well, what are you waiting for? I need your help."

THE DRESS IS STUNNING. I can't deny that. It's not my style, but it is very much Rhian's. It's huge and covered in heavy ivory lace.

"You look like a princess, Aunt Rhi-Rhi," one of Rhian's nieces squeals as she spins around showing off its beauty.

God, there's been so much squealing today I actually have a bit of a dull throb at my temple.

"Okay, people, it's time to move. We want to keep Jack waiting but let's not let him think you're jilting him. Unless you're having second thoughts, Rhi?" I wink. "I know a great place in Lake Tahoe where he'd never find us."

"Funny, but not happening. I can't wait to see him."

"I know." I give her a massive beaming smile. "So let's get you there, bestie."

We all bundle ourselves and Rhian's massive dress into the back of the limo and head towards the church. Her dad died when she was a teenager, so it's her mum who has the pleasure of walking her down the aisle today.

As the limo turns towards the church, I spot a man standing at the entrance, obviously looking out for us. He's wearing the navy suit I helped Rhian pick out for Jack and his groomsmen. It fits him so well it could have been tailored for him. Knowing I'm behind darkened-glass, I make the most of drinking the guy in. I really should have paid more attention to who Jack said was coming to the wedding. It's a shame this dude wasn't at the engagement party. It'd have made that a more fun experience for sure.

The guy's hair is styled perfectly, his chin has just the right amount of scruff, and the way the fabric of the suit pulls across his body makes me think he's hiding something delicious underneath. But what really captures my attention is his eyes. Even from here I lose myself in their blue depths.

"Who is that?" I whisper to Rhian.

"Uh... I don't—Holy shit, that's Brandon."

"No fucking way!" I yell.

Rhian's sister tuts, making a show of covering her daughters' ears, but both of us are too distracted by the man standing at the entrance to care.

"Jack said they'd Queer Eye-ed him, but I didn't think for even a second that that was hiding behind all that hair."

"No, me either. It can't be him. He's too... too... fit," I admit. My interest is evident in my breathy voice.

"I thought copping off with the best man would be a little too cliché for you." She laughs.

"Who mentioned copping off? I'm just appreciating what God gave him, that's all. It's amazing what washing and grooming can do for a guy."

I'm completely and utterly speechless at the transformation.

"Yeah but now he's all neat and tidy, just how you like 'em. Anyway, how long's it been since a guy saw what God gave you?"

My cheeks heat because it's been longer than I want to admit.

"Long enough."

Thankfully, we pull up in front of the church then and the subject is swiftly forgotten.

3

BRANDON

I THOUGHT weddings were all about the bride?

Ever since I turned up at the church it's been. "Is that YOU, Brandon?" It got to the point where I could see Jack was getting pissed off as it was supposed to be about him and Rhian. But he started it. He was the one insisted on my man makeover so it's not my fault people are obsessed with asking me about it.

I only had my hair and beard trimmed for God's sake. I've not had cosmetic surgery.

I'm ecstatic when the bride arrives and the wedding starts, then it's all about them. I watch as Rhian comes walking up the aisle. Jack is beaming at her while simultaneously shaking like a leaf and his eyes are wet. She's beaming right back at him.

She looks beautiful, albeit dressed in this over the top flouncy stuff women insist on putting on for these things so they look like princess dolls instead of human beings. Like for instance Rhian's fully made-up and has her hair in ringlets. She's never looked like this before in her life, but I guess that's why it's called a woman's 'big day'. Pull out all the stops time.

I realise then I could be talking about myself. I'm preened and in a suit. I have also never looked like this in my life. Fucking Jack.

My eyes centre on Reese behind the bride. She's helping to carry the bride's train along with a little girl either side. I have to confess that she looks amazing. It's a shame I only have the front view because I'm wondering if she's having a Pippa Middleton moment and if her arse looks mighty fine. I realise while I'm staring at her that she's staring back at me, but for once it's not with disdain. It's like she's... hungry... and I'm food. What the actual fuck?

I'm distracted and busy as I perform my best man duties and even my locked-up heart softens a little as it watches the true love before my eyes as my best friend and his fiancée are pronounced husband and wife.

Signing the register puts me in close proximity to Reese. The woman is actually a bit of a babe. It's a shame she's such a cow.

Now I keep seeing her look at me. It's a proper head-to-toe perusal like she's mapping my frikking genetics or something. She walks over to me and knocks a piece of fluff off my shoulder. It gets my back up. She needs to keep her judgy hands to herself. I've always been too polite to say anything to her though for in case I should upset her, but maybe today, with my new look, I should develop a new persona to go with the look? What is it women seem to like? A Player? A Bad Boy?

A few drinks down me and I reckon I could go for it at the reception. See what reaction I get from the women who keep flirting with me. Tonight I might get laid! I have a hotel room where the reception is being held so why not? In the meantime, I think I'll wind Reese up; revenge for her treating me like shit before.

I turn to her. "Any excuse to get your hands on me, huh?"

I watch and I've got to say it's thoroughly enjoyable as her eyes widen and her lips part. Miss 'I'm always in control' Connors is a little lost for words right now.

"You had fluff on your arm. We don't want it spoiling the wedding photos, do we?" she says icily, but I can see I've actually rattled her cage.

Registers are signed, and then it's time for the photos. Great. I hate having my photo taken and here comes Reese again.

"You're welcome, by the way," she says.

"Sorry?"

"For your makeover. You actually look like a human being. But I know you'll be too proud to thank me, so I'll just pretend you did. So again, you're welcome."

I decide to call her bluff.

"Actually, yes. Where are my manners? Thank you, Reese, for getting Jack to make me over. I've been a little low for a long while now and hadn't realised the rut I was in. Now I feel I can start to get my life back on track, plus looks like I'm going to get laid tonight. And it's all thanks to you. I'm sorry I can't repay the favour, only personality transplants aren't available yet, but I'll start a regular savings account, just in case."

She stomps off in a huff and then I laugh because she has to come back for some more photos.

The wedding photos take ninety minutes. I'm

bored out of my brain. Now it's time to go to the hotel and enjoy the sit-down meal and then there's still the evening reception. I check my watch. It's four thirty. At what time might I escape this torture? I vow to never get married, or if I do, it's a quick register office thing. No, I'll go back to my original thought not to bother. I like my solo life. Constantly having someone telling me what to do, or picking fluff off me. No thanks. Actually, tonight I'm going mean boy, to put all interested females off. Sod having a shag, I'm going to get drunk and sleep by myself like usual. These women here never wanted to know me before, when I looked a bit on the scruffy side, did they? I realise that's not a fair argument as I was a bit of a smelly boy, but still, I'm totally being judged on my appearance right now. I'm being objectified.

Finally, the evening reception gets under way, and tons more people have arrived, which means in another hour or so I can escape to my room. I've had quite a bit to drink now because women keep buying me a pint.

It's ridiculous. The meaner I am, the more they won't go away.

"Hi there." A blonde sidles over to me, her

green eyes twinkling. "I'm Amber, Rhian's cousin. It's nice to meet you…"

"Don." I've got to the stage where I can't be bothered to say my whole name anymore.

I shake her hand, but she doesn't let go, just kind of lets my hand slide out of hers. "So would you like to dance, Don?"

"No, thank you."

Amber looks a little put out that I'm rejecting her. Doesn't stop her from moving closer to me. "Gosh, it's warm in here isn't it?" She adjusts her top so more of her boobs are showing. Earlier in the night this behaviour made me quite excited, but now it's on repeat, I'm getting bored. "I'm a little thirsty…"

"Well the bar's over there." I point to where I've sent at least eight women tonight so far. They still don't get the hint though. This is why I'm a bit pissed.

"Oh yeah, let me buy you a drink. Pint of beer, right?"

"I'm fine."

"No, I insist."

They all insist.

While I'm waiting for Amber to return, my eyes alight on Reese. I see her shake off a guy's hands from her arse. Looks like he won't take no for an answer. I might not like the woman but she's my best mate's sister and blokes shouldn't behave like that anyway. Forgetting all about Amber, I head over to where they are standing.

"Problem?"

"Yeah, you're here," the guy says. "We're busy, so why don't you go back to where you came from?"

I stand up straighter and flex my fists. "Well, because for one thing the woman you're hitting on is the groom's sister, so if you don't back off you're going to end up in deep shit from most of the people in this room, and mainly because that's my wife you're trying to get off with."

Reese's eyes go wide and then she plays along. "I tried to tell him, honey, but he wouldn't let me get a word in edgeways."

"Take a fucking hike before I knock your teeth down your throat," I tell the guy.

I'm making this shit up as I go along and I don't even care. Never hit a bloke in my life. If he comes at me though it's true that most of the people here would come to my aid. But I'm pissed from all this beer and finding it hard to give a toss.

The guy holds his hands up. "Okay, mate.

Backing off. Sorry. Didn't see a ring and she didn't mention a husband." He basically runs away and I start laughing.

Those icy eyes are looking at me, narrowed. "What's going on with you? You're different."

"You know nothing about me, Reese, so how would you know I'm different? The most communication there's been between me and you over the years has been your judgy looks in my direction, and your occasional twatty comments, so how about you just thank me for getting rid of that dickhead instead of starting twenty questions when you've never given a shit before."

She's silent for a few moments and then she surprises me. "I'm sorry, Brandon. You're right. Thanks for getting rid of him for me. He didn't understand I wasn't interested."

"What? Thought he could thaw the Ice Queen? As if."

Oh dear. I see I've fucked up as her jaw sets taut. "You don't know me either, so how about you just take your own assumptions and stick them up your arse."

She looks so haughty. Haughty and hot. Fuck, I really have had a lot to drink. "Listen, if I promise not to insult you and you promise not to insult me, how about we stick together for the rest of the night, so we don't get hit on by idiots? Unless of course there are any you're interested in?"

"No. I just want to enjoy my brother's wedding. As much as you can enjoy any wedding."

"Right? Bloody tedious things. Put me off marriage for life."

"Huh, you want to do my job, now that would put you off marriage for life."

"Let me go get us both a drink, and let's drink to the happiness of your brother while vowing to never ever be so stupid as to get married ourselves."

We drink to that and to a lot of other things.

"Fuck, I can hardly stand up," I slur. "Whattimesit? Can I be released and go find my hotel room now?"

Reese is swaying around and singing. I watch her hips move and imagine them moving against me. She looks pretty in her bridesmaids dress and with the alcohol loosening her up she seems almost... human.

"It's time for bed," Reese sings. "Let's go and say goodbye to Wedding Loser Central." She looks at her watch and tries to stand still to see the time. "I think it's ten to twelve." She says just before the

DJ announces it is indeed ten to midnight and almost Christmas Day.

"I want to open my presents," she says excitedly. "They're in my room. Did you bring yours?"

"No. Why would I want to drag what I know is socks and crap aftershave with me? I'll open them when I get home."

"Come to my room please and sit with me while I open my presents?" She grabs my arm and begs. "Only Rhian and Jack have hijacked Christmas, They've made it all about them instead of about presents."

"Another reason to not get married. It ruins Christmas!"

"Yes!"

We wander out of the room and eventually find our way to the right hotel room after getting out of the lift on the wrong floor twice. After several attempts to get the key card to flash green, I follow Reese into her room.

She falls onto her bed where there are a pile of presents, and she pats the space at the side of her.

"Sit. Sit."

I basically faceplant onto the bed and Reese starts giggling. "Be serious," she says while laughing. "It's Christmas and I want to open my presents."

I sit up and watch as Reese opens her gifts. Boring undies that she pulls a face at. Perfume she doesn't like. Books she says she doesn't have time to read. Jewellery she doesn't like.

"I don't think anyone knows me at all," she says sadly.

I lift up her chin. "Hey. It's just Christmas. You buy what you think a person will like and they never like it at all. It's as stupid as weddings. So just tell me what you actually want for Christmas and I'll buy it or give it to you. It's much easier if you tell people. Okay, it's not a surprise then but at least you're not disappointed. Like I want a bottle of whisky, so you can just buy me one sometime."

"Okay, done. Now what do I want for Christmas. Ooh I know," she says, her eyebrow rising. "I want your cock inside me. That's what I want for Christmas."

Did I say her telling me what she wanted wouldn't be a surprise?

"But we don't like each other."

"So, let's have some downright dirty hate sex," she suggests her eyebrows wiggling suggestively.

It's still one hell of a surprise. But do you know what? I'm totally up for getting up.

"Take your dress off," I order. I'm going to rock Reese's world… as soon as I can manage to get my own trousers off.

4

REESE

MY HEAD'S spinning too much to really think about what I've just asked of Brandon. We've spent the whole day enduring the pleasantries of a wedding when we should have been celebrating the holidays. I've had to turn away one too many guys who thought it was their right to hit on the single bridesmaid and I'm so fucking pissed I can barely see straight. So logically, what I need right now is some hot and dirty sex with a guy I hardly know and barely even like.

He doesn't even bat an eyelid when I tell him I want his cock inside me for Christmas. This Brandon is different to the yeti-like quiet guy I remember Jack introducing me to a few years ago. I make a mental note to ask my brother if he's sure this man staring at me like he's about to devour me is actually the same man.

"Take your dress off," he demands and I scramble to get off the bed. My foot gets caught in my ridiculously long and lacy dress and I go flying towards the floor.

"Ow," I cry, lifting myself up but I'm stopped when a warm pair of hands land on my shoulders. His lips press against the sensitive skin beneath my ear and my entire body shudders. Goosebumps prick my skin as his fingers find the top of my zip and he begins pulling it down.

The fabric is pushed from my shoulders, exposing my tan strapless bra. He flicks the clasp and it immediately falls away from my body. My breasts are heavy with need.

"Brandon," I moan, needing more than this.

"Lie back."

I do as I'm told, my back pressing against the rough carpet as he pulls his tie from his neck and makes quick work of removing his shirt, shoes, socks, and trousers, leaving him standing above me in just his black boxer briefs.

My eyes drop to his chest and abs, showing me that I was right when I first saw him this morning.

He was hiding something impressive under that suit. Not bad for a yeti.

Pushing my thighs wide, he drops to his knees. His hands run up my legs, pushing up the mass of fabric as he does so, while his mouth drops to my nipple. He sucks and nips, driving me crazy. My core floods, soaking my lace thong and making me desperate for what he promised me.

"Fuck," he grunts when his fingers find the wet fabric and he wastes no time in pushing it to the side so he can find my clit.

"Oooooh, yes," I cry, thrusting my hips to try to get more.

Today's been tedious as fuck and I need this release as much as I need my next breath.

His fingers drop lower, finding my entrance and he plunges them inside me as deep as they'll go. My pussy clamps down trying to suck him deeper.

"Greedy bitch." I shiver when his breath coats my neck as he trails kisses up towards my ear. "You need my cock, don't you?"

"Yes, yes," I chant.

When his fingers slip from me, I almost cry out in frustration, but when I look down and I find him pulling his cock out, the words die on my lips.

Instead, I bite down on my bottom one and watch as he pumps his length a couple of times.

"Condom?" he asks, his eyes wide in panic.

"My bag, pass my bag."

The second he hands it over, I hurriedly turn it upside down and shake until the contents are in a pile on the floor next to me. Plucking a square packet from the pile, I thrust it towards him.

In seconds he's rolled it down his length and he's nudging at my entrance.

"Just fuck me," I demand when he spends way too long teasing me. I don't need teasing, I need action and an earth-shattering release; if he's capable of it.

"Of course I'm fucking capable."

My lips snap shut, not realising I voiced that concern out loud.

"Need proof?"

I open my mouth to reply, but he chooses that moment to thrust forward, filling me almost to the point of pain.

"Fuck." My arms fly above my head until I find the wall. I place my palms flat against the smooth surface and brace myself for what I think is to come.

And I'm not disappointed.

Brandon ploughs into me over and over again. My legs tremble, my breasts bounce, and my cries and demands for more get louder and louder.

Needing more, he slips his hands under my arse and lifts me just so. The angle is everything I need myself and after two more hard thrusts, I cry out his name as I fall over the edge.

"Brandon, fuck." My pussy clenches around him as his own moans of pleasure fall from his lips.

"Fuck. Fuck. Fuuuuck." His body stills above me as his cock twitches violently inside me.

Why did I ever think he was pathetic and useless?

"Because you're a judgemental, stuck-up bitch. But I won't hold it against you because you're a stellar lay."

"Shit, I didn't mean—" Fucking alcohol. I can't tell what I'm thinking and what I'm speaking out loud. Oh well, who cares, I'm having an amazing time.

"S'all good. I got what I needed." The wink that follows that douchebag sentence pisses me off as much as it turns me on. His softening cock slips from me and he stands, pulling the condom off and dropping it into the bin.

"That's all you need?" I goad him. "Maybe you weren't the man I needed for the job."

"Oh I'm man enough. Get up."

Pushing to my feet, I allow my dress to drop to the floor before shoving my knickers down my legs. With my shoes still on, I stand just an inch or two shorter than Brandon. My eyes hold his, the alcohol running through my veins makes focusing hard, but my determination to get what I need overpowers it.

"Show me what you got, big man."

His hands land on my waist and I'm thrown onto the bed like nothing more than a rag doll. He drags me onto my hands and knees and takes me from behind, pushing inside me hard and holding onto my breasts, squeezing. His thrusts have my head banging occasionally against the headboard but I don't even care.

I just want him to keep doing what he's doing because it's not just Christmas that's coming.

WHEN I WAKE and roll over the next morning, I don't know what hurts more, my head or my aching muscles.

What the fuck happened last night?

The last thing I remember was drinking with Bran—fuck, Brandon.

Sitting up so fast, my stomach churns and my head spins, but when I look to the space beside me, it's empty.

"Shit." Dropping my pounding head into my hands I try to recall the events of the night before. Little flashbacks start hitting me. Sex on the floor, on the bed, against the wall on the way to the bathroom, in the shower. Fuck, no wonder my muscles hurt.

My need for the bathroom eventually gets the better of me and I swing my legs from the bed.

"Ew, what the—" Looking down at the floor, I find a used condom stuck to the bottom of my foot. "Ew, ew." I shake it until it flies off. Vowing to come straight back and tidy this place up, I make my way to the bathroom. I want to scrub my foot off.

I do my thing and quickly discover how sore I am down there after the events of last night, before standing at the basin and risking a look in the mirror.

My eyes widen and the limited content of my stomach threatens to make itself known when I get a look at myself. My hair looks like a bird's nesting in it, my make-up's smeared all over my face, and I've got fucking love bites all over my neck and chest. Who leaves fucking loves bites these days? We're not twelve.

Reaching for my cleanser, I pump a generous amount into my hand and set about fixing my face.

By the time I emerge from the bathroom, having performed my exact morning routine even with a hangover, I look a little more respectable. Within five minutes the room doesn't look like a tornado blew through it last night. I'm expected to attend a family Christmas breakfast in the restaurant downstairs in twenty minutes, so I try to ignore the pounding pain in my head, and the memories that keep trying to relive themselves.

I blow dry my hair, reapply my make-up that I hope goes some way to covering the giant circles under my eyes and the glowing red marks I can't cover with my blouse, and swallow two paracetamols, although I might just go for some more alcohol and hair of the dog.

Slipping my feet into my shoes, I suck in a deep breath, preparing to look into his knowing eyes.

IT APPEARS everyone's already seated when I walk into the restaurant and I curse myself for not being on time.

I'm never late. I'm always on top of things and the first to turn up, always. This is his fault.

My eyes scan the room so that I can ensure I don't accidentally sit next to him, but I don't find him there at all.

"Reese, over here," Rhian calls, distracting me. I walk towards her, glancing at the two empty chairs and praying one isn't waiting for Brandon.

"Morning, 'wife'."

"Eeeek," she squeals. "I'm a wife and he's my husband." Jack turns and nuzzles her neck. His eyes find mine and I just about manage not to puke in my mouth at the sparkle in them. I do not want to think about the fact that I wasn't the only one testing out the many surfaces the hotel rooms had to offer.

"My eyes. My eyes," I moan.

Rhian rolls hers but thankfully removes her new husband from her neck so we can catch up.

"So what happened to you last night? I came to find you to say thank you for everything and you'd disappeared."

"I... uh... I had one too many and took myself to bed."

"Alone?"

My stomach twists. I don't lie to my best friend, but this is one truth that I think is probably best I took to my grave. "Of course. By the time I'd had a couple of losers hit on me, I wanted to be on my own."

Her eyes narrow at me. She's not buying any of this. She knows me too well. I need a swift change of subject.

"So was it everything you dreamt it would be?"

"And so much more. It was beyond perfect. He's beyond perfect," she coos.

Shoving my fingers in my mouth, I make a show of how that kind of confession makes me feel about my big brother.

Rhian chats away about how incredible yesterday was and I can't help feeling like we could well have been at two different events. Nothing about yesterday made me want to follow their lead down the aisle, but listening to her animatedly reliving it, you'd think it would convince anyone to tie the knot.

When I think enough time has passed to ask

without looking suspicious, I turn to Jack. "Where's your best man this morning?"

"Your guess is as good as mine. That seat right next to you is reserved for him. He probably spent the whole night shagging. Whoever the lucky lady is has me to thank for it you know? I made him look like that."

"Do you feel okay, Reese? You look a bit green." Rhian looks at me concerned.

"I'm fine. Just had one too many, you know?" I reply, wondering how cocky my brother would be if right now I thanked him for my sore vagina.

5

BRANDON

IT'S the wedding breakfast and Christmas Day.

I don't want to go downstairs.

Would they believe me if I faked my own death? I feel 95% dead with this hangover anyway.

Jesus Christ, I fucked my best mate's sister at his own wedding reception, and I didn't just do it once. Oh no, I kept repeating my asshole mistake over and over and over.

And it was so goooood.

Shut up brain! Not helping.

I feel like the biggest shit for leaving while she was sleeping but I figured we both needed some processing time before we had to see each other again.

Having thrown myself through the shower and

still feeling like absolute hell, I dress in jeans and the Christmas jumper Jack is forcing me to wear for his breakfast. There's no escaping it any longer; plus, I think a cooked breakfast will help considerably.

Walking into the breakfast room, I scrub a hand through my now much shorter hair which just doesn't give the same amount of comfort as being able to hide behind the previous long locks. I'm immediately struck by the severe lack of Christmas jumpers amongst those attending. All of those seated stare at me. All of them.

Jack bellows with laughter and points to a seat. "I was joking when I said we were wearing Christmas jumpers, you great idiot."

Fuck my life. If I had the energy, I'd kill the newlywed. I decide that I can look like an idiot or I can adopt my 'player' persona again and make out this was my plan all along.

I look at my captive audience. "So I know this breakfast is to further celebrate the joyful union of Jack and Rhian. However, it is Christmas Day." I twirl around in my jumper and wiggle my arse for full effect. "So to that end it's time for the ladies to all receive a present from me."

Even though my head is banging, I grab a piece

of mistletoe off the table and I walk around to every woman there and give them a Christmas kiss.

Everything is fine until I head towards the bride. There is just her and the other woman I have yet to look in the face left.

I lower myself towards Rhian. "Step away from my wife." Jack laughs.

"Sorry, mate. This is my revenge for the whole jumper thing. I'm stealing a kiss from your beloved." I kiss her cheek. Rhian giggles.

Then I head towards my seat and my eyes lock onto Reese. She's so tense, and her pallor wears the look of the severely hungover. She looks more like a waxwork than she does herself. I swoop down to kiss her cheek.

"And you can definitely keep your distance from my sister," Jack yells.

I smile at him as I kiss her cheek. "Merry Christmas, darlin'." I wink at Jack.

"Seriously, you've had your fun now." Jack half-jokes.

I hold my hands up and take my seat. "I'm done. Time for me to fill up on breakfast."

"You're looking a bit pleased with yourself. Did you score last night?" Rhian asks, a glint in her eye.

"Me? No. Was too plastered to do anything but fall into my own bed," I lie.

The breakfast is awkward given that Reese makes no effort to talk to me whatsoever. She doesn't even ask me to pass the butter or anything. When Rhian calls her on it, she just offers the excuse of a hangover. It's extremely obvious that in the cold light of day Reese Connors does not want to acknowledge what happened the night before (and some of the morning after). *Or maybe she just wants to talk to you after in private,* I consider.

I carry on eating my fill of breakfast and start to feel much better.

"You should have stayed the extra night with us all," Rhian complains. "It's not too late to add it, you know?"

"No can do. I'm working Boxing Day evening. The sales will have started; it'll be really busy."

"Yeah, all the sad fuckers who want to buy half-price Christmas crackers for next year." Reese finally breaks her silence. "I mean, what is wrong with people?"

"They're skint?" I counter.

Reese shrugs. "So don't buy any at all."

"But they want a nice Christmas next year, so they're doing it on a budget."

"They might have money by next Christmas. In the meantime, they've got to store Christmas Crackers for a whole year. Is it even worth it?"

"Well, obviously it is to some people. Those who want to give their family a lovely Christmas."

"Just saying I don't get it."

"Well, you have money and you don't have kids so why would you?"

The moment the words are out of my mouth I want to eat them back, but it's too late. Cutlery clatters onto her plate as she pushes back her chair. Then I can see the fight on her face as she picks her cutlery up and puts it on her plate to show she's finished and wipes her mouth on a napkin. She just cannot lose the stick up her arse. Then she stalks out of the room.

I look at a horrified Rhian and Jack.

"I'll go apologise. I'm sorry. She just pushed my buttons."

Last night she was helping me unbutton them. I much preferred that.

I catch her in the hotel foyer. "Hey, Reese. Wait up. I'm sorry."

She swivels around and that ice-cold stare is back. "No, I'm sorry. Sorry I had too much alcohol and slept with a loser like you. What the fuck was I thinking?"

"I'm not a loser." She's pissing me off now.

"They had to do a pity makeover on you because you were too embarrassing to have at the wedding like you were."

That hits hard. I know it's not completely true. My mate was trying to help me because I have let myself slide, but it still cuts.

"Well, I think we can safely say that last night was a mistake to never be spoken about again," I say.

"Yep, as far as I'm concerned it never happened. Luckily, the fact I was drunk means I've blocked most of it from my mind anyway."

"I'll be civil to you at family events but other than that my time trying to be polite to you is done. Bye, Ice Queen."

I turn away from her before she has a chance to add any further insults and make my way to my room to pack. I can't get out of here fast enough. My mouth curls up in a smirk at the fact she has another entire boring day of wedding celebrations to suffer through while I'm out of here.

When I arrive home, I change out of my jeans and Christmas jumper. My parents live down

South and I've arranged to see them over the New Year. The house is tidy and lacks any Christmas décor other than the small pile of presents next to the fireplace and the pile of received cards stacked on the coffee table that I can't be bothered to put up. I make a coffee and open my gifts. As I thought it's just the usual aftershave, ties, and socks. Once I've finished my drink I sigh and look around. Now what do I do with myself? Flicking the TV channels and finding nothing of interest, I decide to go back to bed.

I may spend a little time thinking about my antics with the Ice Queen, but in my mind I can forget she's a bitch.

One month later

IT'S the end of January. I made a New Year's Resolution to keep my new image intact and to keep the house tidy; the latter because of looking for a new roomie. Unfortunately, I've yet to find anyone suitable to house share with, but I'll keep trying. At least the fact I have my savings means that I can be fussy for another couple of months.

Appearance wise, it's been much easier to keep my new look due to the amount of women it's attracted. I've been dating over the last month. My new appearance has given me a confidence I'd been lacking before.

The more I've thought about it, the more I've realised I've been in some kind of funk for a while. Well no more. Women like Reese are not going to be able to judge me and think I'm some kind of slobby loser. I'm going to show that cow in particular. Her snobbiness has spurred me on in some weird way. I feel uber competitive. She might have the smarts in that she's a hotshot lawyer, but that doesn't mean I'm some dumb arse because I didn't fly through my exams.

The fact is, I did carpentry at college and have made things for the house on occasion. I've never done much with my skills because I got the job at the warehouse and got comfy. But now I'm done with playing safe. It's time for a change. Over the last month, I've cleared the garage out and set it up, ready to start some carpentry. I thought I'd start with some tables and benches and set up an Etsy shop online. For now, it'll be a hobby but I'm going to see where it takes me. Maybe I'll become self-employed and own my own business? Then I'll make a wooden dildo for Miss Reese Connors to stick up her arse, although that space is no doubt already occupied by a stick.

The thing that annoys me more than anything in the universe is that I can't forget the sex. I might have been drunk but for the most part I remember that it was so damn good. I need to get her out of my mind and so for that I need to meet other women.

I'm on the cusp of change and it's glorious. I'm finding my groove and not only in the wood I'm handling. Oh for God's sake. I think of handling wood and then I'm picturing my cock in my hand as I drive it into Reese's pussy.

I will get that annoying woman out of my head. I will.

6

―――

REESE

"I JUST DIDN'T EXPECT any of this," Mrs Harper sobs across from me in my office.

"I know. It all must have come as a terrible shock. But I can assure you that we'll fight for everything you deserve."

"My parents told me not to marry him," she cries. "But he seemed so perfect for me. Made me promises that I believed he would keep. I never thought he would cheat. And with our nanny."

I pass over a couple more tissues as she cries for everything that bastard did to her.

"Trust me, Mrs Harper. We'll—"

"It's Vivian, please."

"Okay, Vivian. You just focus on yourself and

the kids. Leave everything else to me and I'll make sure he regrets ever betraying you."

"Thank you, Reese. I don't know what I'd do without you." She reaches a hand out and squeezes mine.

When I first started this job, I thought dealing with emotional clients would be the hard part, but I find sympathising with them remarkably easy, and seemingly I'm good at it if my reputation and success rate is anything to go by.

"Oh I'm so sorry, I've gone over our time once again. I do apologise for making you late."

"It's really no problem. My priority is you right now." It's not entirely true, I'm due in a meeting that was meant to start twenty minutes ago that could determine my future success at the company, but I can hardly throw a sobbing woman out of my office. My boss will understand.

Mrs Harper gathers her stuff, and with a few more sniffles, she heads out of my office to attempt to restart her life.

I grab my laptop and diary and run for the meeting room.

All chatter ceases when I step into the room.

"My apologies. I had a meeting with a client overrun." I aim my apology at Clive, our managing partner but I quickly glance at Rich and Harriet too.

They all nod their acceptance and I rush to take a seat.

My head's still with Mrs Harper so I mostly miss the first part of the meeting; that is until Clive starts talking about restructuring. He discusses which job roles are likely to go but more importantly he moves onto what could affect me.

"As you're already aware, we're looking to take on a new partner. I already have a good idea in my mind as to who would be a good fit, but we will be setting up meetings with everyone involved in the restructuring in due course."

Dragging my eyes from my boss, they lock with Rich's who's directly opposite me. His eyes narrow, assessing me just as much as I am him. It's obvious that we'll be at the top of the list for that partner role. We've both been here the longest and have the best reputations. But as much as I might want it, I know that I'm younger with less experience than him. That doesn't mean I'm not going to fight like hell for it though. I believe I deserve it and I'm not going to shy away from proving my worth. Plus, I know secretly I'm Clive's favourite. He's told me on more than one occasion of how I remind him of how he was in his early days.

"That position's mine and you know it," Rich whispers in my ear as we make our way out of the meeting.

"Tell yourself whatever helps you to sleep at night. But I've got as much chance as you and you know it. You're just threatened because I'm younger than you as well as being a woman."

"It's mine, Connors. So don't be too disappointed and try to smile like you're happy for me when it's announced." Rich disappears into his office, leaving me seething. He knows damn well that I'm just as good, if not better than him.

As usual, I work much later than I should. By the time I shut my computer down and walk out of the office I'm the only one left. I can't be the only one in this office without a family to head home to, but it seems that everyone else, including Rich, isn't as dedicated. Surely that should help tip the scales in my direction?

I stop at my favourite deli on my way home and pick up something quick for dinner, and of course a cupcake for dessert. I'm usually all for vanilla, but for some reason I didn't fancy that today and went for chocolate. I've got a fully functional kitchen in my apartment; it was one of the reasons I chose the place, but the oven is as clean as it was the day I moved in.

Flicking on lights, I drop my bags to the counter ready to dish up before heading to my room to get a little more comfortable.

Slipping off my shoes, I place them inside the floor to ceiling rack in my walk-in wardrobe before stripping off my black pencil skirt and red blouse. I fold both and then place them into the laundry basket ready to be collected.

Pulling on a cami and a black pair of leggings, I wrap a cashmere shawl around my shoulders and walk into the en suite.

My steps falter when I see the box I left abandoned last night after chickening out. I managed to put it out of my mind at work like I do everything in my private life, but now I'm home my situation seems more pressing than ever. It's not even really a situation. My unreliable body has tricked me before now and I'm sure it'll do it again. But my period's almost two weeks late now, so I really do need to find out if I have an issue.

Shrugging off the shawl, I allow it to drop to the floor before stepping forward and ripping open the box like it's a plaster I need off my skin.

I'll just pee on this thing, find out my body's just screwing me for shits and giggles and move on with my life; hopefully, as the newest partner at Mortimer and Jones.

Before I even sit down, I can't help but pick up the shawl and hang it on the back of the door. I can't look at that mess while I wait to see the negative sign.

Happy that everything is in its place, I rip the foil packet and set about following the instructions.

Putting the toilet lid down, I sit back on it and stare at the stick in my hand.

The line appears telling me that it's worked. My heart pounds and my hands tremble as I wait to see what happens in the other window. I've no idea why I'm nervous. There's no way I'm pregnant.

Laughing at my crazy thoughts, I allow my mind to wander back to my only sexual experience in the past six months. Brandon fucking Weston. Why out of all the men I've been with over the years has it got to be him who gives me a serious false alarm?

I check my watch before I look back at the

stick. It's been over four minutes now. The result should be clear.

I'm already ready to throw the offending stick in the bin as I look down at it, expecting to see one line in the window.

I have to do a double take. My legs betray me and I fall back down onto the toilet with a bump.

"No, no, no." This test must be wrong.

Reaching for the box, I check the expiration date. *Still over a year's life on it.* "Fuck."

My hand shakes so violently that I drop the fucking stick and end up on my hands and knees trying to retrieve it from behind the toilet.

This can't be happening to me. And with that fucking hobo.

Jesus, I'm going to give birth to a yeti.

Dropping the test and the packaging into the bin, I turn to wash my hands. It's only when I glance at myself in the mirror that I realise I've got tears running down my cheeks.

What the hell do I do now? I'm meant to be preparing for a promotion, not a nursery.

"Fuuuuuccck," I scream into my empty apartment.

Wiping at my face, I collect my shawl with the

intention of continuing with my evening as planned.

I dish up my salad and pop my pre-prepared salmon in the microwave. The smell makes me heave and makes me think of the other times this has happened in the last couple of days.

The thought has fire burning through my veins. I'm nowhere near prepared to deal with something as life changing as this right now.

My life is planned, well thought out, and organised to a point it could be considered compulsive. An unexpected pregnancy was not part of my life plan. There's no way I can be a single mum and a kickass family lawyer. The two do not mix.

Unwrapping my fish, I place it next to my salad and carry it, along with a glass of water, over to my dining table while I try not to breathe through my nose.

I pop a tomato into my mouth, but I don't taste it at all. I'm too busy trying to work out where my life started going in a different direction than instructed. The image of Brandon standing outside the church the day of Rhian and Jack's wedding pops into my head and I know it's all his fault.

Why did I think sleeping with that waste of space would ever be a good thing?

I've no idea how long I sit there staring at my long gone cold salmon, but eventually my need to talk to someone gets the better of me. Usually my go to would be Rhian. She understands me and doesn't judge how I live my life, but I can't go to her with this right now. She won't be able to keep it from Jack and he'll probably run straight around to Brandon's to give him the good news. No, I need someone who's miles away and not likely to spill my secret before I figure out what the hell I'm going to do.

"Jesus, Reese, do you know what time it is?" Sarah, my oldest friend says groggily. "Just because you can run on two hours sleep, it doesn't mean everyone can."

"I'm pregnant," I blurt, unable to keep the words in.

"Holy fuck. I'm awake."

Sarah and I have been friends since we were born, our mothers being friends for even longer. They still joke that if one of us was a boy we'd be married with three kids by now.

It's not true. Sarah and I couldn't be more different if we tried. Although I guess both our jobs are done with a similar focus in minds, kids' welfare. She's currently a nanny for a rich family up in the Lake District looking after three little devil kids if her stories are anything to go by. She tells me she loves it, but it sounds like a living hell to me.

"What am I going to do?"

"I've no idea, Reese. That's kinda down to you, and the dad. Ooooh who's the dad?"

I groan as I picture him once again. He'd probably be Sarah's perfect type, which means he's everything that isn't mine.

Fuck my life.

"A hobo."

Sarah snorts her shock. "I'm going to take that as a joke because I know you have much higher standards than fucking an actual hobo."

"He's Jack's best friend. I fucked him the night of his and Rhian's wedding. I planned on never thinking about it ever again but—"

"But now you're growing his spawn."

"Not helping," I warn, much to her amusement. "Now I'm ringing for sympathy so come on, give me some."

"Okay. Let me get comfy and then you can tell me everything."

By the time I put the phone down, I realise that although I enjoyed a catch up with my friend and an opportunity to purge my current circumstances down the phone, I'm no further forward with the dilemma facing me right now.

I'm pregnant and it's my brother's best friend's. I need my cupcake.

7

———————

BRANDON

February

THE DIFFERENCE A COUPLE of weeks makes. Armed with my newfound confidence, not only have I made and sold quite a few items of handmade furniture with a very healthy mark-up, but I've also been on more dates, and today I handed in my notice at work. One more month of night shifts and then I'm done. I've also decided not to get a new housemate. If I'm going to be working days and having dates, I want to be able to bring women back to my now immaculate pad, plus be able to work on my business without worrying about someone else being in the house. I mean... what if they were untidy?!!!

I laugh to myself. Poor Aiden. I'm making that guy whatever piece of furniture he desires because I realise I owe him big time. I'd invited him around for a pint tonight, but he'd refused. Because it's Valentine's Day. Ugh.

I've received three cards, which is three more than in the last three years to be honest. My last date had tried to get me to take her out again tonight but no way. I am not about to go all hearts and flowers. I did all that with my ex-Naomi. Been there, done that. No woman is going to break my heart again like she did. Not anytime soon anyway. I'm having a fab time. My dick is having an even greater time, and my heart is being kept in a locked cage for now. Maybe one day the right woman might come along and I could learn to trust and love again. But I'm living the dream right now. I have my own shag pad and my own business. My appearance might have changed, but I'm not sure I recognise myself right now anyway!

There's just one problem if I'm going to be brutally honest though: right now I'm bloody knackered. I'm shagging, making, working, cleaning, and my sleeping hours are cut right back.

I no longer have time to nap on a sofa. There's always something to do. However, my life is better for it so I shall persevere so I can live the dream, even if I can't sleep and dream.

However, it is Valentine's night, so I'm not going out. The idea of a night alone appeals more than I want to admit. To have a bit of a rest from my new life and say hi to my long-lost friend the sofa. I stick a pizza in the oven and put on some comfy loungewear: shorts and a long sleeve top.

No sooner is my arse sat at my dining table then the doorbell goes. Who the fuck could that be? Annoyed, I get up and head to the front door, ready to tell whichever salesperson it is to piss off.

But I find Reese standing at the other side of the door.

I'm immediately suspicious because she's not wearing her Ice Queen look. Instead, she looks... friendly and... nervous. These are not emotions I associate with Jack's sister so loud alarm bells ring in my head.

Why would Reese be here on Valentine's Day?

Oh... I get it. She's not got a date and she's realised that my dick is talented. She's come for some more sugar. I'll let her squirm for it.

"Can I come in, Brandon, please? It's about what happened between us at the wedding."

"Absolutely. Come in. I'm just grabbing a bite to eat." Calm down, Brandon. Play it cool.

"Oh, is it a bad time? I can come back. I drove here so..."

"It's not a bad time. I'm just eating. Come in and give me five minutes and then we can... get to what's on your mind."

She follows me into the kitchen and immediately I see her turn her face up at my pizza like she's going to puke.

"Sorry, it's not what you posh birds eat, but I'm having a rare night off. I've been very busy of late."

"It's not that, it's—"

"Yes?"

"I'm just not feeling so good."

Now I'm confused. Why has she come to see me for a shag if she's not well? Is she not here for that? Has something happened to my best mate?

"Is Jack okay?" I double check.

She shrugs. "He was the last time I spoke to him. Too busy in the honeymoon stage to bother with me much right now." She pauses. "Would it be okay if I waited in your living room until you've eaten?"

Hmmm, maybe this is an excuse for her to go strip off in there and then when I follow in later she'll be laid tantalisingly on the sofa?

"Sure. I won't be a minute. Would you like a drink?"

"Maybe a glass of water?"

"Okay. I'll be through shortly."

It's only at that point, when she's gone that I remember I'm in my pyjamas. As I look down I see my dick has been proudly displaying its girth under my shorts the whole time. Damn beige material. Oh well, she's seen the real thing and hopefully they'll be off in a minute.

When I walk into the living room, I'm unprepared for what I'm looking at. For some reason Reese is kneeling on my sofa with her head and half her torso leaning over the back of it. Her skirt has risen up showing her thighs. It's the strangest 'take me' sexy position I've ever seen, but I'm not *that* experienced in women's seduction techniques so maybe she's going to teach me something new. Walking over I slide my hand up her thigh.

She turns back to me and everything happens at once.

There's a feral looking woman with something

unidentifiable running from her mouth glaring at me.

The stench of something rotting hits my nostrils.

The sharp sting of a slap to my face is felt before my head ricochets a little.

I fall to the floor and start heaving myself.

"What in God's name is going on?" I groan, then heave again.

"I've been sick, you fucking idiot. I couldn't see a bin, so I just aimed for the back of the sofa. Where are your cleaning things? I'll get it cleaned straight up. Oh how gross." She looks scathingly at me trying not to bring my pizza back up.

I shake my head at her. "You're not well. You sit down and I'll see to it."

Her hands go to her hips and her face relaxes before she bursts into a fit of giggles.

"You're going to clean up my vomit? You can't even get your hand away from your face."

I try to remove it to prove otherwise but it's no good. I start to almost barf. "For fuck's sake, Brandon. Go back to the kitchen and show me where everything is," she orders.

She's just been ill and now she looks perfectly all right. She really is some kind of fucking robot. I follow her into the kitchen—thankful beyond words to get out of the living room—and watch as she rinses her mouth under the tap and then starts opening cupboards and getting cleaning materials out. Meanwhile I sit back at my dining room table and try to find something else to think about other than Reese's vomit.

The whisky calls from the inbuilt kitchen wine rack. Dragging in deep breaths I take a tumbler from behind a cupboard door and then pour myself a decent measure and enjoy the burn as a mouthful coats my throat. The fine aroma gives my nostrils a different smell to imprint on my brain rather than the vomit one.

Reese walks back in with a carrier bag full of kitchen towel and wet cloths. "All done. I'll just take these to your outside bin. I'll replace anything I've used. Hopefully the smell will completely disappear, but if not, get your carpet cleaned and send me the invoice, although actually, it's partly your fault so maybe I'll just leave it to you."

It's partly my fault she puked? Is she going to blame having to look at my face or something?

She goes outside and I hear a bin clatter and then she walks back into the kitchen. Her face goes a bit green again. "Erm, can we go somewhere else to talk? I can't stay here with the pizza smell."

"And I can't sit in my living room with your vomit smell, so that leaves my bedroom. Please do not puke in there."

"Show me where the bathroom is and we'll be fine."

We walk upstairs and I push open my bedroom door beckoning her inside. I see her eyes noting everything as she walks in and sits on the end of the bed. I sit next to her. This is really turning out to be a strange evening.

"I can't believe you tried to hit on me while I was being sick," she states.

"You turn up at my house on Valentine's and I find you with your arse in the air bent over on my sofa. What else is a guy to think?"

She ponders my answer for a moment.

"Fair enough."

"So why are you here? I've wracked my brains and gone through you wanting a repeat performance, my best friend having died, and now I'm coming up empty because why would you come here if you were ill? I'm confused."

"I'm pregnant," she says.

I swallow hard because I am sure she just said that she was pregnant. Then I stare at her.

"Excuse me?"

"I'm pregnant, Brandon. That's why I'm here and why I've puked over the back of your sofa. It's why I pulled a face at your meal. Not because I'm a snob over pizza. I actually usually love pizza. Just not the smell of it at the moment." She takes a deep exhale and I can tell that whatever I choose to say next, she feels a sense of relief that her pregnancy news is out in the open.

Baby daddy informed. Tick.

Baby daddy having a humongous panic attack? Not sure she saw that one coming. My breath is coming in short, sharp gasps. The walls are closing in. I CANNOT BREATHE.

"I'm dying." I gasp. "Quick, record me." I pant. "I leave everything to my unborn child."

What I am not expecting is her to slap my face again.

I sit back shocked clutching at my throbbing cheek.

"Get it together. I know it's a shock, but you aren't going to die. Now I'll let you off today but being able to deal with puke might be featuring in your future life. I'm keeping the baby. I wanted you to know that whatever your own parenting decision is, I'm having my baby."

"Okay." I nod. I'm finding it difficult to say anything else.

"You're okay with my decision to keep it? Not that it would change anything anyway."

I carry on nodding.

"So we'll need to talk about my upcoming first scan and whether or not you want to be at all the appointments. How we'll co-parent, how much visitation you'll want etc. I know it's all a shock and early days so how about I leave you to process the fact you're going to be a dad around September time and I come back to see you tomorrow night?"

Again I can do nothing more than nod.

Reese stands up. As she walks past me, I hold out a hand near to her stomach and then I pull it away again.

"It's okay," she says. She grabs hold of my hand and brings it to her stomach. I feel the warmth of her skin through my fingers, the soft cotton of her top.

"I don't think it even has ears yet, but 'hey, bean. This is your daddy'." A moment passes between us and then she bids me goodbye and says she'll catch up with me tomorrow.

I'm vaguely aware of the downstairs door closing and then I hear a car engine fire up.

How did it happen? Well I know the whys but we used... oh fuck. We had sex over and over and over. I don't remember if condoms were involved every time, given I was so very, very drunk.

My mobile phone beeps and I take it out of my pocket.

Lauren: Booty call? I know you said you didn't want a Valentine? I could come over after midnight?

Booty call? I never want to have sex again. Look what it's done. Thank fuck I know for definite I've used condoms with my other conquests, otherwise I could end up with a whole nursery full.

I sit back and think about how my life just changed with those two words from Reese, and how I didn't just get dodgy looking socks for Christmas after all. I got another present, though it's currently still wrapped up... in Reese's stomach.

8

REESE

I HAD no idea what Brandon was thinking when I walked out of his house the night I told him about my pregnancy. Nothing about that night went as planned, from me emptying the contents of my stomach over the back of his sofa or him having a panic attack when I told him.

After that reaction I was half expecting to never hear from him again, so you could imagine my surprise when a hamper was delivered to my office the next morning full of morning sickness remedies and other horrifying things like nipple cream.

I was busy admiring the contents when Rich came strolling into my room. He must have known something was up by the horrified expression on my face, but he soon moved onto more pressing issues than the hamper I threw under my desk the second he knocked.

I had no idea how I'd managed to keep my pregnancy secret from work because I spent a good chunk of my days in the toilets throwing up.

I've booked today off work, something that hasn't happened... well, ever. I can't even remember the last time I had a holiday, which is pretty pathetic.

I'm sitting in the waiting room surrounded by other pregnant women of varying sizes. I'm trying to keep my eyes to myself, but my curiosity keeps getting the better of me every time a belly walks past me and I start to wonder if I'm going to end up quite so big.

Brandon told me he was coming today when I emailed him with the details. I might have promised him I'd see him the day after my surprise announcement but as usual I ended up stuck at the office and I haven't managed to see him again yet. I think we both can't face the reality of what's happening.

Brandon has been emailing me periodically to find out how I am and if bean is okay, but that's the limit to our relationship, and I'm more than happy with that. I made the decision to continue with this pregnancy for me; I didn't have any unrealistic ideas that we'd suddenly become a happy family. I've no idea how everything is going to work. I'm a self-confessed workaholic who's going to become a single mum.

As the time for my appointment comes and goes, so does my hope that Brandon will be here to see our baby for the first time.

I don't have a lot of patience at a lack of punctuality at the best of times but mix that with pregnancy hormones and my frustration levels soon begin to get the better of me.

"Miss Connors, please."

"Reese, wait," Brandon calls just as I'm about to follow the sonographer into the room. "I'm so sorry, I lost track of time."

My eyes drop from his to take in his paint covered overalls.

"Glad you dressed up for the occasion," I snap, turning away from him and entering the room.

"I didn't think the baby would be all that bothered."

"No, but I have eyes and I'm the one who's got to look at you." I don't mean to sound like a raging bitch, but really, couldn't he have at least had a shower and put some decent clothes on for this?

"Thankfully, I don't really care what you think, Ice Queen."

The sonographer looks between us with a somewhat amused expression at our bickering before instructing me to get up onto the bed and lower my trousers.

Brandon sits himself in the chair next to me and starts to pick at a large blob of paint on his leg while the sonographer gets organised.

"Is that necessary?"

"What? Being here? You were the one who invited me."

"I know why you're here. I'm not likely to forget that drunk decision anytime soon."

Rolling his eyes at me, he goes back to the paint. I've no idea if it's just to wind me up some more, but if it is, it works like a charm.

"Stop it," I snap. "Just frikking stop it." His eyes hold mine and fire burns between us. I can't believe he's the father of my first born. What exactly did I do to deserve this?

Our bickering stops the second the sonographer instructs us to both look at the screen.

"Fuck. That's our baby," Brandon exclaims, his eyes wide as he stares at the fuzzy black image.

"Where? It looks like a broken, old TV."

The sonographer is quick to point out our baby's features and I find that if I squint and turn my head to the side then I can just about make it out.

"Why aren't you crying?" Brandon asks, when the sonographer wipes the gel from my belly and turns to print off our pictures.

The truth is that I'm still a little shocked all of this is happening and although I've made the decision to keep the baby, I don't feel like I've really accepted this is real. Aside from spending an hour or two of my day with my head shoved down a toilet bowl, nothing about my life has changed yet. I've no bump. I don't have any baby stuff in my apartment aside from what Brandon sent me that I've hidden in a cupboard. It all just seems like a dream.

"It's because I'm an Ice Queen, remember?"

"Oh so you're aware that you're a cold-hearted bitch?"

I pin him with my best icy stare as I'm handed back my maternity folder along with the printouts of bean.

"Thank you. Is that all?" I ask the sonographer.

"Yes, that's all for now. As long as everything progresses as it should, we'll see you in about eight weeks. Well, that's assuming you two haven't killed each other by then of course."

"Don't tempt me," Brandon mutters, much to the sonographer's amusement.

"You're both in this together, and it truly is a miracle what you've created. Please try to enjoy it; you'll regret it otherwise."

"I'm certainly regretting drinking too much wine," I mumble, before thanking her and walking from the room.

I don't stop to see if Brandon's following me; I don't really give a shit. I don't slow down at all until I get to my car. I press the button to unlock it and go to open the door when a warm hand lands on my forearm.

"Wait, please." Looking up, I find a soft pair of blue eyes. "I'm sorry. It's just that your judgemental side gets my back up."

"I wasn't judging you. Your paint picking was just really annoying."

"You weren't judging? So you didn't take one look at my clothing and wonder why you didn't fuck a guy who wears a fancy suit other than at weddings?"

"No, I didn't. I was just wound up worrying about whether the baby was okay and panicking you weren't coming, because for some strange reason I actually wanted you there for support." I admit. "But I couldn't cope with the bits of paint going on the clean hospital floor. Someone has to clean up after you, you know? Or someone might get it on their shoes."

"You do know how messy kids are, right?"

"Don't. I know I'm a bit weird with things being tidy, but I just like order."

"Your puke wasn't very tidy. That shit went everywhere."

"I said I'd pay for cleaning. Anyway, what were you doing to get paint all over yourself?"

"Do you fancy getting some lunch? I'll fill you in."

"Uh... sure. Can we get pizza?"

"I thought pizza made you puke?"

"Not anymore. I can't get enough of it now."

"Okay, if my baby wants pizza then that's what my baby shall have." Something weird happens to my insides when he calls me baby. It's too intimate.

"Don't call me that."

His mouth drops open at my cold tone. "Wha—oh. I didn't call you baby, Reese. I meant our actual baby."

My cheeks heat as realisation hits me and I feel ridiculous for jumping to such conclusions, and even stupider for quite liking how it felt when he said it.

"Did you drive?" I ask when the awkward silence between us gets too much.

"No, I got a taxi."

"I guess you'd better get in then."

I drop down into the driver's seat and he makes his way around to the passenger side. He's just about to put his arse on the leather when I panic. "That paint's all dry right?"

"Yeah, Ice Queen. It's all dry."

"Okay, you can sit then."

"What would you have had me do otherwise? Hover?"

I shrug, trying to fight the laugh that wants to bubble up my throat at the thought.

"Watch out, I think your face is about to crack."

I lose the fight and a smile breaks across my face. "Oh fuck off. I do have a sense of humour, you know?"

"Good to know there's one in there somewhere. Hopefully, our baby will inherit mine."

"Our baby," I muse. "I can't believe my baby shares DNA with you."

"I could say the same thing." Silence descends around us as I pull out of the hospital car park. I start to think he's not going to say anything when he asks me a question I've been trying not to think about. "Does Jack know?"

I shake my head. "Only you and my friend Sarah know. I wanted to get through today and make sure everything was okay before announcing it."

"He's going to kill me."

"You're his best friend. I'm sure it'll be fine," I lie.

"Do you have any idea how things work with guys?"

"Why would I know that?"

"There are unwritten rules. You never touch a girl any of your guys have been with without explicit approval beforehand and you most definitely don't touch their sisters."

"Yeah so you tell him, then it's you that gets all the grief. It wouldn't be good for the baby, so I'll pass."

I take him to my new favourite restaurant, Pizza Hut. Now there's something I never thought I'd hear myself say. But their pizza crust along with their 'all you can eat' buffet is exactly what bean wants. And like what Brandon said, what bean wants, bean gets.

We both opt for the buffet and Brandon orders a beer while I'm stuck with lemonade. I'd kill for a glass of Sancerre right about now.

"You ready?" he asks, nodding towards where fresh pizzas have just been brought out.

"So ready."

Together we head over to fill our plates. It's the first time since he arrived at the hospital that we don't argue and it feels... nice.

I grab myself two slices of pepperoni before reaching for the barbeque chicken, but my fingers don't connect with the plastic utensil; instead, it meets a warm, calloused hand.

I look up in shock and my eyes meet his. My surroundings seem to vanish as I lose myself in his intense stare. My heart starts to race and my temperature spikes. I'm reminded of how good it felt to be in his arms that night.

"You can have it."

My brows draw together. Is he offering me a repeat? "Huh?"

"You can have it. The last slice."

When I eventually manage to pull my eyes away from his and look down, I see that there's only one slice of barbeque chicken left.

"Oh... um... no, you can." I stutter, feeling a little flustered by his close proximity all of a sudden.

"No, I insist."

"Th- thank you."

He picks up the slice and deposits it carefully onto my plate before turning to the next pizza on offer and taking the two biggest slices.

I ignore the salad having read about having to make sure it's well washed when you're pregnant and return to the table. The butterflies he kickstarted are still fluttering inside me, but I try to tell myself it's hunger.

"Are you feeling okay?" he asks when he joins me and finds me staring into space.

"Yeah. I'm fine."

"Saying grace or something?"

"No. Just asking myself how I ended up here with you."

"I think it started when you asked for my cock for Christmas."

My cheeks burn and I rush to shove some pizza in my mouth before I say something crazy about not actually regretting it so much any longer.

9

BRANDON

I'M in Pizza Hut eating buffet pizza after seeing my unborn baby on a screen.

"Could I have a look at the scan picture again?" I ask.

"I got two copies, one of them is for you. Sorry, I'm so distracted by everything going on, I forgot."

"Miss Perfectionist isn't perfect? Hang on while I take a photo." I raise a brow.

She holds off going in her bag. "You have me all wrong, you know?"

"So you're not a ballbreaking family lawyer who has everything in her house a certain way and never has a hair out of place?"

"Well... up until I got pregnant maybe. But since I've been puking every day, I have most definitely had my hair out of place. My house is only tidy because I pay a cleaning service because the minute I'm home I'm out like a light. The exhaustion is real. This baby is taking it out of me."

She passes me the photo. It's just a blob on a photo. A 'bean'. But that's my baby. I'm going to be a dad, and something comes over me at that point. Because I know I'd already do anything for that bean. I said I'd never let my heart be broken again, but for bean I'd hack it out of my own chest.

I place it in my pocket carefully.

"So you said you'd explain why you arrived covered in paint?"

"Oh yeah. Well, I left the warehouse job I had and I'm now a full-time carpenter. More than full-time at the moment actually. I'm self-employed and have orders coming out of my ears."

She's actually lost for words I think. She takes a bite of pizza to try to cover it.

"How did you become a carpenter overnight?"

I laugh. "I didn't. I learned at college after school and I got a job with my ex's father's business. When my ex dropped me for her father's main competitor's son, I went off the whole thing. But now I don't need anyone else to work for. I can work from home and take orders online. I thought it would take a while to get going, but to be honest, I might have to close my books for a bit against further orders. I'm that busy."

"Wow. So what sort of things are you making?" she asks, actually looking genuinely interested instead of scornful.

I take out my phone and open up my Etsy page. I show her the carved mirrors, storage boxes, tables, and seating.

"Some things are collection only; others are mailed very well packed."

Her eyes are wide as she scrolls through. "These are absolutely amazing, Brandon. I had no idea."

"No. That's the thing. Everyone just sees me as a nightshift warehouse working slob, and I'll be honest... I was a slob. Life felt easier. It wasn't but it felt it. As for my job, there was absolutely nothing wrong with that job. It was steady, they were a great team. I left because I didn't want to work nights anymore and the makeover your brother started fired something up inside me that I'd thought was dead. Got me excited to try my carpentry again."

"Well, I wish you every success with it all." Reese dabs at her mouth with a napkin.

"You okay so far? Not feeling nauseous?"

She shakes her head. "It tends to hit first thing in a morning and then sometimes again in the early evening. I've been trying ginger biscuits and they're helping, so thanks for the, erm, twelve packets you sent."

"I worked in a warehouse. I'm used to bulk buying."

"This is so weird isn't it? I barely know you and I'm carrying your baby."

"So get to know me. Let's be well... friends."

"Friends?"

"Yes. Let's meet up and do stuff and find out about each other."

"That's great except for the fact I work full-time and then I come home and sleep. I've no time to get to know you."

"So what are you going to do when bean arrives? About work I mean?"

"I get my maternity leave."

"And after?"

"I'll sort some childcare, like all other working single mums have to. My mum isn't near enough so she's out."

"But I am, and I work from home. I can change my hours around to make sure looking after my kid is my number one priority. They'll be spending half the week with me anyway."

I see her bristle. "We've not decided anything about how we're doing this yet."

"It's my baby as much as yours."

She leans on the table, her head in her hands. It's not until I see a tear fall on the table that I realise Ice Queen is either crying or thawing out.

I get up and move around to her side of the table and put my arm around her.

"We'll work it all out," I tell her.

I feel her body shake and her voice comes out trembly. "It's just all too much right now. I feel too tired and sick to think properly. I'm looking at becoming a partner at work and instead of being my usual fabulous self, I'm trying not to let them see me throw up. I'm a mess."

"Come stay with me," I blurt out before my brain can catch up with my mouth.

"W- what?"

"Come move into my house until you feel better. I have a spare room. We can decorate it if you want. I'd decided not to get a housemate, but right now while you're feeling so sick you need a little looking after. So move in. We can get to know each other better then too; in between your working, sleeping, and puking."

She shakes her head. "I can't do that. That's the most ridiculous idea I ever heard."

"Why is it? I'm your baby's father. Makes perfect sense to me. But then again, you're a snobby cow so my place probably isn't good enough for you, right?" I'm back to wanting to throttle her.

"Yeah, that's why I'm saying no. Not because I barely know you, but because your house isn't as upmarket as mine. Maybe if you put a red carpet down at the front door, I'll consider it." She's staring at me with that icy gaze and then I get an eye roll to boot.

I try to keep my patience. "Just think about it okay? Don't dismiss it outright. You only have to slum it until you feel better. Then you can fuck right off." Ooops, patience has left the building.

"Can you not swear in front of the baby?" She pats her stomach. "I'm sorry, bean. Daddy has a filthy mouth."

"Yeah, bean, which is one of the reasons you got there in the first place," I quip.

I don't miss Reese squeezing her thighs together.

She takes a deep breath. "It's my birthday on

Sunday. Jack and Rhian have insisted on throwing a family lunch at theirs. I've just decided I'm going to announce my pregnancy. Do you want to be there? We could try to be civil while we announce the happy news. Let them see we are determined to co-parent and put the baby first."

"You've decided this just now, in the fifteen minutes we've eaten pizza?"

"Yup, might as well get it over with and you're no doubt too chicken to tell him."

"I'll be there. What time?" Damn my ego, why didn't I let her tell him and then emigrate while it was happening?

"The meals at one pm."

"I'll come around at about three. Then we can tell them together."

She nods "Okay, something we agree on at last."

We say our goodbyes and I head home where I spend the rest of the day staring at the photo of my baby.

SUNDAY ROLLS around fast and before I know it I'm knocking on Jack's door. Jack of course has no idea that I'm coming.

"Hey, mate. I wasn't expecting you, was I?"

I shake my head.

"Is it urgent, only the family are round. We're celebrating Reese's birthday."

"Can I come in and then I'll explain?"

"Erm, okay, mate." He stands back and lets me pass through. He then notices I've a wrapped box in my hand.

"Brandon." Reese says as she looks up from the dining table where she's stuffing her face with what looks like a pink-iced cupcake. "Hello."

"Oh hi, Brandon." Their mum, Laura, says. "Good to see you again."

"Looking good, son." Their father says. I see the side-eye from Laura. They try to be civil when with their kids, but they loathe each other.

"Happy birthday." I pass Reese the box.

"Thank you. I'll er, open it in a moment. Everyone. There's something I'm wanting to say to you. Well, actually, we, me and Brandon, want to say to you."

I look at Jack and he's gone a bit pale.

"You are not dating. Please tell me that you are not dating," he yells.

"That's not the announcement." Reese answers.

"Phew. Thank God for that. So, I'm guessing a business partnership of some kind? Some law and carpentry mash up. Can't solve your family disputes, buy a handmade weapon," he jokes. Then he shuts up as no one else is responding.

"We're pregnant," Reese announces. "Brandon and I are having a baby."

There's a moment of complete silence and then Jack is out of his seat and he manages to get me to the floor, his fist flying into my jaw hard before his father drags him away.

"You've done what?" Jack yells. "You've taken advantage of my sister and got her pregnant? You fucking bastard. Well, you can damn well marry her now. Oh my God, I'm going to fucking KILL YOU."

"Jack, darling, your sister just announced we're going to be grandparents, can you calm yourself?"

"She's shagged his mate," Jack's dad, Pete reminds her. "I seem to recall you not being so calm when I shagged yours."

"Yes, well, in the end I realised she did me a favour."

"Oh, here we go."

"This is going well," Reese states. We watch as Rhian drags Jack over to the corner of the room for what looks like a lecture and their parents stand bickering.

It's time for action, although I decide it's better that we lie. I grab Reese's hand.

"Excuse me. Could you all come back to the table please for a moment?" Everyone hesitates. "Now," I order. Reluctantly, everyone makes their way back and takes their seats.

"So Reese and I have been on a couple of dates after meeting up again at the wedding." I stare at Reese and she nods enthusiastically, obviously agreeing this is a better way to play it.

"Anyway, we've been a little taken by surprise by current events. But we are both pleased and excited about the baby and we've agreed to carry on dating and getting to know each other and see where it goes. Our baby is our priority and should we decide to just remain friends, we will co-parent." I pause for breath. "I appreciate this is a huge shock. It was for us too, but we would like it if you could join in our celebrations as you are going to be Uncle Jack, Auntie Rhian, Grandma Laura, and Grandad Pete." I tenderly stroke Reese's stomach and she puts her hand over mine. Fuck, I actually genuinely feel a bit emosh.

"Well, I'm a firm believer that things happen for a reason," Laura says. She walks up to her daughter. "If you're happy, we're happy, darling. I can't say it isn't a shock. We didn't actually think you'd ever even have a family, you seemed so career focused, but well, we know Brandon is a lovely boy." She turns to me. "Who seems to finally be getting his lazy arse in gear. So, congratulations, though I'd like to be a Nan please, Grandma sounds so old." She wraps her daughter in a massive hug and Reese bursts into tears.

"Congratulations," Rhian adds. "I think it might take your brother a little longer to get used to the idea, but he will, won't you, Jack?"

"We'll be having words." He levels at me. I'd be happy with words. Trouble is I think each one is going to be accompanied by some knuckle action.

Reese gets the scan photo of the baby out to show everyone and as the women and her dad get a little teary, I hand her the box with her gift in. She takes off the lid and inside finds a hand-carved photo frame, just the right size for the scan picture.

"Oh, Brandon. It's perfect," she says, and she takes the photo and slips it inside.

I take her father to one side and reaffirm my intention to do the best I can for Reese and the baby.

"I know you will, Brandon. I've known you a long time and I know you're a good man. You lost your way a bit but now you're on a new path. Parenthood doesn't come with a book, my man. We're all winging it all the way. Just do your very best. That's all we ask. And I know she's my daughter, but if she ends up like her mum, I'll understand if you split up."

"And that's my cue to leave," Laura says. "Congratulations once more. Happy birthday, and thank you, Rhian, for the beautiful lunch." She kisses her son, daughter, daughter-in-law, and me, and then tells Pete she hopes he drops dead.

"Do you need a lift home?" Reese asks me.

"No. I drove, but thanks."

Once we've said goodbye to everyone, I help Reese carry the remaining cupcakes that she apparently had instead of a birthday cake to her car.

I stand at the side of her driver's door and I hand her another small box.

"Another gift?" She says surprised.

Removing the lid, inside she finds a key attached to a wooden keyring. The keyring says Baby Mama on it.

She looks up at me.

"It's a spare key to my house. If you need to stay for any reason. Need someone to hold the sick bucket etc. You just let yourself in. My casa is your casa."

"Thank you. I appreciate it." She yawns. "Anyway, it's been a bit of a heavy day, so I'm going to head home to bed. My birthday present to myself is sleep!"

"Okay. Well you know where I am," I tell her.

I watch as she drives away and then feeling eyes on me I look at the window of Jack's house where Jack does the 'my eyes are watching you' gesture obviously having learned it from Aiden before Rhian drags him away from the window mouthing 'sorry'.

REESE

March

FOUR DAYS after my birthday and one of my clients decides against turning up for her appointment. I take it as a sign to take my exhausted body home for a change instead of working myself until I'm almost asleep at my desk like every other night.

I get strange looks as I pass everyone else's office. I don't think I've ever left this early, which is saying something because it's coming up for six o'clock already. Most normal people are probably already at home making dinner and planning what they're going to watch on TV.

Ignoring their stares, I make my way home—via the deli of course. What I really want is pizza, but I already had a takeaway over the weekend. I might be pregnant, but I can't just keep eating, keep using it as an excuse to pig out. I'll be the one who has to deal with the baby weight once I've given birth.

Given birth. The thought sends a shiver down my spine. I don't have the first clue about what to expect during labour, what the pain relief options are, what the best position is for the baby. Pulling my phone from my pocket, I order myself a book that I hope will give me all the answers.

I've placed my shopping down on the counter, then made it to the bedroom and have my blouse undone when a weird noise sounds out. It's not weird per se, but it's not a sound I hear every night of the week, or ever really.

Thinking the only reason someone could be ringing my buzzer is because there's an emergency, I forego pulling on another top and head for the door.

Pressing down the button, the little screen comes to life and I find someone I really wasn't expecting standing in front of the camera.

"Reese?" he asks, leaning in a little.

"Holy shit, have you got a black eye?"

"How about you let me in, and I'll explain. I have pizza." He holds up a box and my stomach rumbles right on cue. *How did he know?*

"Of course, come on in."

He chuckles but doesn't say anything about me clearly wanting to invite the pizza in more than I did him.

I've got the door open and I'm waiting for him. I smell him before I see him—well, the pizza—thankfully Brandon is still the clean and scrubbed up version of himself that got me into this mess in the first place.

"Gimme gimmie." My fingers reach out for the box, but he holds it slightly out of reach.

"Uh, Reese, did you forget something?"

His eyes drop from my face in favour of my breasts and I'm reminded of my half-dressed state and my practically see-through lace bra that's almost on full display.

"Fuck. I'm sorry."

"You don't ever need to apologise for flashing me your tits."

"You're a pig."

"Maybe, but I'm a pig with pizza."

"Set it up over there. I'll be right back." I point towards the breakfast bar and race towards the bedroom to cover up. I've no idea what he thinks about this place. He probably hates it, with everything in its rightful place, but I don't give a shit. This is my home, not his.

I quickly change into a silk pair of pyjamas and throw my cashmere shawl over my shoulders. Double checking myself in the mirror, I head out to devour the pizza he brought over.

"I bought it for us to share you know?" Brandon complains when I pick up the last slice without checking to see if he wants it.

"But it's for the baby." I shrug. A smile pulls at his lips and the simple move has something fluttering inside me.

You're just horny. It's the hormones, a little voice says in my head but I'm not so sure I believe her.

"So tell me about the black eye," I demand, trying to distract myself from the way his t-shirt pulls across his chest.

"Ah, courtesy of your brother."

"Jack hit you... again?"

"Yeah, he really hasn't got over the idea that I shagged his sister yet. I thought a couple of days would have been enough for him to cool off. Apparently not." I raise an eyebrow for him to explain. "I went around with beer before last night's game, but I didn't even make it until half-time. I think you should probably talk to him. At least he can't hit you."

I KNEW Jack wouldn't be all that happy with how things had developed between Brandon and I but the last thing I expected him to do was lash out and punch his best friend... twice.

"I will. I'll call him tomorrow. Rhian said he was still pissed but I didn't know it was to that extent," I say nodding towards his eye. "Does it hurt?"

"Why, are you going to nurse me back to health? You know, I really could use a gentle touch right now."

I blow out an exasperated sigh. "If this," I say waving my hand over the now empty pizza box, "was all just a way to try to get me back into bed then you really needn't have bothered."

His eyes light up like I'm about to make that exact suggestion.

"No, you should have stayed at home. I'm not making that mistake twice. This might turn into twins."

"I'm not sure it works that way, Reese." The amusement on his face pisses me off.

"No? Well, I'm not sure using condoms is meant to work quite like this either."

"Touché."

Brandon leaves not long after our little spat. He tries to find out if I'm going to be home early any other night. Something inside me longs to tell him that I'll be here every night, but I know it's the wrong thing to say. Instead, I agree to meet him for coffee in a few days' time and bid him goodnight.

When I fall into bed my belly is full of gorgeous pizza, but I can't get the man who provided it out of my head. Reaching for my bedside table, I take matters into my own hands. Who needs a man anyway?

***

"GOOD AFTERNOON," Chantelle, Clive's assistant, sings as I walk towards her desk. Today's D-day as far as who's being made partner. We were meant to find out weeks ago, but Clive had a heart scare and ended up in hospital, so everything ground to a halt. I still haven't decided if that was a good thing or not. I might not be spending half my days in the toilets now but because my fate is yet to be sealed as far as my job goes, I've kept my pregnancy secret, or at least I hope I have.

I should have told them by now, but I didn't want my situation affecting their decision. Just because I'm having a baby it doesn't mean I won't be able to do my job. I deserve this promotion; I've worked my arse off for it.

"Reese, come and have a seat. Would you like a coffee?" Clive asks.

"Actually, a glass of water would be great, thank you."

Chantelle goes running off to get our drinks and I take a seat in front of his desk.

Clive pushes some paper around, refusing to meet my eyes and my stomach twists. He doesn't get nervous. He's one of the best lawyers I know, so his hesitation right now has panic zipping around in my stomach.

He doesn't look up at me until Chantelle has been and gone with our drinks. Then he takes a large breath and drags his eyes from the wooden desk.

"Reese, you are a fantastic lawyer. I knew the moment you walked into my office that you were going to be an asset to the company."

I wait for the 'but'.

"But—"

There it is. Oh fuck.

"As you know, we've had to re-evaluate things after my little stay in hospital. I was forced to make some decisions that I didn't think I ever would." The look on his face isn't one that leads me to believe he's about to give me a promotion. "I'm so sorry, Reese, but we're going to have to let you go."

My world tilts on its axis as blood rushes past my ears, meaning I don't hear another word that Clive says.

We're letting you go. We're letting you go. Those four little words repeat in my mind over and over as the room I'm in spins and I struggle to catch my breath.

"Reese? Reese? Fuck, she's totally out of it."

The concerned voice confuses the fuck out of me. Where am I?

My eyes flutter open and I take in the dark red carpet beneath me and the shiny black shoes that are next to my head.

Looking up, I find the concerned faces of my boss and his assistant.

Why am I on the floor?

We're letting you go.

Sitting bolt upright, my eyes widen to the point I worry they might pop out of my head as I try to gather my thoughts.

"That was a dream, right? You're not really getting rid of me... are you?"

I go to stand and Chantelle races to reach out and help me up.

"I'm really sorry, Reese. The decision is out of my hands."

"How? Why me? What about Rich? Hey, did he tell you I'm pregnant? He saw my hamper, didn't he?"

I see the truth on Clive's face. He knew all right. His mouth opens before he snaps it shut again.

"You should sit down. Here, drink this." Chantelle thrusts my glass into my hand. "Are you feeling okay?"

I've never passed out before in my life but that isn't my biggest concern right this second.

"Clive?" All the blood has drained from his face as he stares at me.

"I'm so sorry, Reese. Here are the details of your redundancy." With that said, he marches from the room, leaving me with a glass of water in my trembling hand and Chantelle looking like she wants to be anywhere but here.

I focus on my breathing for fear of passing out again.

"Right... well..." Standing, I place the glass on the edge of Clive's desk, pick up the brown envelope, and march out of his office with my head held high.

Walking through to my desk, I focus on my breathing so I can manage to calmly ask my assistant to cancel all my appointments today. I tell her I have a migraine and that I'm going home. I don't hang around my office long enough for her to ask any questions.

I feel sick and don't know if it's pregnancy related or stress related. Although the women's bathroom is closer, I pop into Rich's empty office and let the contents of my stomach empty into his waste bin. Then with my bag over my shoulder, I walk out of our offices. My legs seem to have a mind of their own as they walk in the opposite direction to the car park and I just keep going.

My mind is numb as I walk down streets I've

never seen before. Eventually, the sun begins to set and the temperature drops. When I recognise a shiver running down my spine, I figure I should try to work out where the hell I am and how to get home.

Home. Why do I suddenly not want to be there?

Flagging down a taxi, I rattle off an address I wasn't expecting to fall from my lips when he asks for my destination. Up until now I'd yet to have a reason to use the key Brandon gave me. To be honest, I couldn't really think of a time I ever would. I've been fine by myself since I left home, other than calling Sarah for advice every now and then. I'm not a person who relies on others, because experience has shown me that they let you down. But then again, I also didn't think I'd be losing my job. A successful career is the only thing I've ever truly wanted in my life and I thought I had it. Now my new reality is that in a few months' time I'm going to be a single mum and unemployed.

Why didn't I save more money when I had the chance? I wonder, thinking about my wardrobes full of Jimmy Choos and Prada handbags. My baby isn't going to impressed with any of that. It's just going to want food and somewhere to live. *What the fuck is going to happen now?*

I pass the driver some money when he pulls up outside Brandon's house and I get out before I have a chance to second guess myself.

I need someone right now and for some weird reason, it's him.

I knock on his front door and wait.

Nothing happens but there are lights on. Maybe he's just working in the garage?

Digging in the bottom of my bag, I pull out the gorgeous handcrafted keyring he gave me. Then I push the key into the lock and let myself in. It feels weird but this is what he gave it to me for. I call out his name but there's no response, so placing my bag down in the unit in the hallway, I walk towards the kitchen. It's empty. The place is in silence, so I wonder if he isn't here after all.

A few more seconds pass but then I hear a noise. Heading towards where it came from, I round the corner into the living room and immediately freeze when my eyes land on two figures on the sofa.

"Oh fuck." Tears fill my eyes and my heart races to the point it actually hurts.

Brandon lifts his head from the woman's neck.

She's wrapped around him like a fucking snake, her skirt pushed up around her waist. Other than that, it seems they're both fully clothed, but only just.

"I'm so sorry. I should have called ahead. Oh shit."

Spinning on my heels, I run from the house.

"Reese, wait," Brandon calls, his footsteps getting closer.

I've just pulled the door open when he catches up to me. His warm hand wraps around my forearm and I still.

"Don't go." I don't like the roughness to his voice that the woman who's probably still laid out on his sofa caused. Something I don't like bubbles up in my belly and makes my eyes burn even more.

"No, you're busy. It's okay."

I go to step forward, but his grip tightens and he pulls me to face him. His eyes widen and his chin drops when he gets a look at my face.

"Reese, what's wrong?"

"It's..." My chin wobbles as I fight to get the words out without totally breaking down. "It's nothing. I'll leave you to... *that*. Maybe call me when you have a few minutes?"

I go to step away and this time he lets me,

although I can tell by the conflicted look on his face that he's not happy about it.

"Brandon?" a female voice purrs from the living room doorway and my stomach turns over.

He looks between the two of us before nodding at me. "Are you sure you're okay?"

"Yes, yes." I shake my hand at him. "Go see to your guest, she'll be wondering what's happening."

"Look, I'll just deal with, erm, this, and I'll call you later, okay?"

The second he shuts his front door, a sob bubbles up my throat.

Can today get any worse?

I hurry until I'm a few streets away from his house and then it takes forever to find an available taxi. By the time I get home I can hardly keep my eyes open. Dragging my exhausted body up to my flat almost takes more energy than I have. I practically fall through the front door, drop my bag to the floor and head straight for my bedroom. Basically the sooner this day ends the better. Sleep can't come fast enough.

I pull off my loose-fitting dress, that I hoped covered my small bump at work, in favour of a pair of maternity leggings, and t-shirt with preggers written across the front that was in the hamper. It wasn't so long ago that I wouldn't have been seen dead in something like this. But right now, I really don't give a fuck. The most important thing is my baby, and he or she couldn't give a crap about what I'm wearing.

Pulling the duvet back, I crawl between the covers and curl myself up into a ball. It's only then, when I'm alone in the safety of my apartment, that I let it all out.

I cry for what I've lost. I've worked myself to the bone for that company and when things get hard it seems I'm the first to go. I cry for the clients I've made promises to and I cry for all the promises I've made my unborn baby that I'm not going to be able to fulfil without a well-paid job. But most of all I cry because of Brandon. We'd not talked about us dating or even about what might or might not happen between us. But seeing him with someone else... well, it hurt more than I ever thought it would.

I'm just drifting off to sleep when I hear something. Turning over, I try to drag myself back to consciousness.

"Reese? Come on, open up. Please. I need to know that you're okay."

Fuck, Brandon is at my door.

11

BRANDON

"REESE? Come on, open up. Please. I need to know that you're okay."

I'm banging on her door and I don't care if the whole block comes out to see what's happening. Why did I let her go upset? What the hell is wrong with me? Why didn't I get her to wait inside? I called a cab for my date and then came straight here because I'm a complete moron.

Eventually she opens her door and a red-rimmed, puffy-eyed Reese opens it. She's wearing the top I got her that says preggers and is just so un-Reese like but sweet.

"Reese, I'm so sorry." I step forward and clasp her in my arms. "What the hell happened? Is the baby all right? I'm sorry about tonight. I wasn't expecting to see you and it threw me for a loop."

She nods and a large exhale leaves me. "Yeah, the baby is fine. But I wasn't and for some reason I just thought you'd be the one who might understand everything that's happening to me, because I'm struggling."

"Come on. Let's go sit down and you can tell me what's going on. Unless you need to rest, in which case I'll wait down here for you while you sleep. Just tell me what you need."

I'm not expecting her answer.

"I need you, Brandon. It must be the hormones. Please?"

She looks so vulnerable in that moment. So not the Ice Queen and I wonder when the icy mask started and who Reese Connors really is underneath it all. She's thawing in front of my eyes, and me, well, I'm currently drowning in her. I pick her up and carry her towards her bedroom.

After laying her in her bed, I quickly strip out of my clothes and climb in beside her under the sheets. I remove her top revealing her pink rosebud nipples on perfect breasts. Reaching a hand to touch them, she says, "Be gentle. They're really sensitive and a little sore."

"Okay."

Leaving her breasts, I reach for the waistband of her leggings and pull them down and off. Lying at the side of her I run my fingertips between her legs. She's soaking and gasps as I touch her.

She's so ready. I ask her to move so her back is to me. That way I can hold her breasts so they don't move too much and hurt. I position myself behind her and then I push inside. She pushes back against me. She's so wet I slide inside her with ease. Her breath hitches and soft mewls escape her mouth as she begs me to fuck her. I'm not one of those men who thinks my cock will touch the baby's head but I am mindful that I want to be gentle, so I move in and out of her slowly. It's exquisite. Usually my fucking is fast and hard, a means to an end, but right now I'm savouring the moment and listening to how much pleasure I seem to be bringing this woman.

Reese moves my hand from her right breast and guides me down to between her legs. I stroke her clit as I move a little faster inside her. She starts to moan and writhe back and I guess she's getting near her climax. So am I. I quicken things up a little and thrust a bit harder while I strum her clit and then she bucks against me as a hard climax squeezes my cock and sets me off. I release my load inside of her, pumping until I'm spent.

She sags back against me. "Thank you, Brandon. You've no idea how much I needed that."

"My pleasure. Use me for sex all you like." I laugh.

Pulling out of her, I head to her en suite to clean myself up. When I return she's fast asleep.

I've still no idea what upset her so much, but for now I climb in at the side of her, deciding to stay so that in the morning I can make sure she's okay.

Are you sure that's all that's happening here, Brandon? I ask myself.

But the truth is I don't know what the hell is going on right now.

WHEN I WAKE up the next morning there's no one at the side of me. I panic that she's gone to work and left me in her apartment alone, but then I hear the sound of someone moving around and a low bass hum from music playing. I dress quickly, visit the en suite to freshen up and go in search of Reese. My eyes take in the apartment in the light of day. It's immaculate, apart from the bed I just vacated. There are bottles lined up on her dressing table. Her nightclothes folded and resting on her pillow. Her perfume hangs in the air.

She's in the kitchen, sitting at a high gloss countertop island with a slice of toast and a glass of water.

"Morning. Any chance of a coffee?"

"Morning. Sure, I've a machine. Let me put a pod in. Latte okay?"

"Fantastic."

It's all very polite and not the conversation you'd expect of two people having a baby or two people who just fucked. I decide to focus on discussing what was wrong yesterday.

I climb up onto a stool and watch as she makes my drink. She places it in front of me on a coaster and sits back on her own stool facing me.

"If you want some breakfast, I can make you toast?"

I shake my head. "I'm good, thanks. I'll grab something on my way home."

She nods, then looks away.

"What happened yesterday?"

Her cheeks heat.

"Not last night, but why were you so upset?"

She sighs. "I got made redundant and I'm positive it's because I'm pregnant."

I'm genuinely shocked. "You lost your job? But you said you were being lined up to be made a partner?"

She shrugs. "I thought so, but yesterday something changed. The boss let me go."

"Can't you take them to court?"

She shakes her head sadly. "No, because I'd not told anyone I was pregnant, so I can't say that's the reason. They found a way to get rid of me anyway. I suppose at least I have some redundancy money to tide me over, although God knows what I'm going to do. I'm unemployed and pregnant."

Oh fuck. I put a hand over my mouth, then drop it. "I sent you the morning sickness parcel to work. I'm so sorry. It's just that's the only place I expected you to be able to accept delivery. Did someone see it?"

"It doesn't matter now, does it?"

I reach out and take her hand. "I'm glad you came to me. That you felt you could reach out to me."

She snatches her hand back.

"Yes, well, that didn't go as I expected seeing as I found you all over another woman."

I scratch the stubble on my chin.

"The thing is… we haven't really defined what we are, and so I was continuing to date. But after last night…"

It's like I can see the ice set around her body as she tenses. "Nothing's changed. I was in need of an orgasm and you provided it. Carry on dating."

I bite on my lip for a moment before releasing it with a pop. "But I don't want to."

"Y- you don't?" Reese looks vulnerable again. I'm beginning to see that the Ice Queen is a protection mechanism for the real woman underneath.

"No. I want to get to know my baby mama and satisfy any urges she might have." I waggle my brows at her.

"So… we could be friends with benefits?"

I nod. "Yep, for now. Friends with benefits sounds good."

She smiles and I notice once more how damn beautiful she is.

"Now. I know you didn't seem keen on the idea, but let the lease go on this apartment and come move in with me. Let me look after you and your needs and then we can take care of our baby together. Once things are a little more settled after the baby's born then by all means move back out if that's what you want. But for now, please move in, although I have no idea where we're going to put a baby AND your shoe and bag collection."

"Okay."

"Pardon?" I can't quite believe that she's agreeing.

"Okay, I'll move in. The thought of having someone look after me and potentially give me an endless supply of orgasms is too good to turn down right now."

I laugh. "You want to move in because of my cock?"

She laughs as well. "Well it is a pretty perfect cock."

We agree that I'll sort out some packing boxes and we'll move her in slowly over the next few days.

"God, what is Jack going to say? He's still being a bit off about the whole thing." Reese's lips turn down.

"Jack can't accept his kid sister has grown up. I'll talk to him. Let's not tell him we're fuck buddies, hey? As far as everyone else is concerned, we're madly in love and have moved in together, ready for our journey to parenthood."

"Okay. I can do that. I can pretend to be madly in love with you. It's worth it to shut Jack up and my parents will feel happier."

I feel unsettled and can't explain it. Maybe it's all the acting? I'm fed up of pretending to be this lothario stud. When I brought that woman back to mine last night, I was just about to stop things and ask her to go home anyway. This whole 'player' act is childish and ridiculous. I just want to be myself, albeit a clean version. Inviting Reese to live with me is a way to put being a 'player' back in his box and nail the damn thing shut once and for all.

"Once we're settled in a week or so, why don't we invite Jack and Rhian for dinner? Let them see we're okay?" I suggest.

"You just want me fawning over you all night." She giggles.

"Hey, I'll have to do the same with you. Ohh, I know! We need to think of pet names for each other."

"Hmmm, yours can be snookums." She's laughing even harder now.

"Oh yeah, well you're now known as cupcake." She snorts.

"So, cupcake. I'm going to grab some breakfast

and some packing boxes and I'll be back later. Okay?"

"Okay, snookums." That's it. A bout of complete hysteria sets in. I leave with Reese having tears down her face again, but this time from laughter.

OVER THE COURSE of the next few days Reese moves in. One thing becomes very apparent. She has far too much 'stuff'. Her shoe and bag collections are vast. Her clothes could fill a whole room (which they did in her apartment as she had a walk-in wardrobe), but there just isn't that room here at mine. With me having items of completed furniture in the house too, something needs to happen and fast.

"This mess is giving me palpitations," she confesses.

"Look, you are going to have to get used to things not being perfect soon. Kids are kind of messy things."

"Yeah, I know." She looks at her belongings. "I'm going to have to sell some of these things though, aren't I?" She pouts.

"It might not be a bad idea."

Reese is sat curled up on the living room sofa. It took a professional cleaning service to get rid of the vomit smell and staining from behind the sofa and I thank God that she seems to be past the puking stage now she's thirteen weeks pregnant.

She taps into the laptop on her knee. "I've sold a few things on eBay in the past. I'll do that again. Then anything I make I can add to my redundancy money for me and the baby."

"Once you've got rid of some of this stuff, we'll ask your brother around, but I want us to look more settled before that happens. I'll get to the post office today myself with all these orders I have ready. I'm going to pick up a lockable storage unit for outside. That way, once I have orders complete, they can wait there instead of in the house. That'll make things even tidier."

It was strange having Reese share my bed at night. We had yet to have sex again, but I kept waking up to find us snuggled close. My feelings were all over the place. Was I in lust, or falling for my baby mama? Whichever, for now things were best staying as they were. We didn't need love complicating things.

12

REESE

WAKING up in Brandon's house with him in bed beside me that first morning was bizarre. But strangely enough, it also just felt right. It was that feeling that had me swinging my legs out of bed to get away from him.

I didn't need to be getting attached to him. That was sure to end in disaster. The sooner I could get a new bed delivered and move into his spare room the better.

His presence and kindness is fucking about with my pregnancy hormones and making me think crazy thoughts about our future.

We don't have a future. We're just being civil for the sake of our unborn child.

Once I've eaten, I sit on the floor in what will

soon be mine and the baby's room—that is once I've got rid of some of this stuff. I didn't think I had all that much when it was all housed in my walk-in wardrobe. But seeing it all here in boxes, I'm actually a little embarrassed by the amount. I'm also ashamed that I spent most of my hard-earned money on all this shit when I could have put it to much better use. I could have bought my own place instead of spending out crazy amounts each month on my rent. I could have invested for my future. But no. All I've got for my years of work are a few designer items that I'm now listing on eBay for a fraction of what I paid for them.

"I'm sorry, bean. I promise to be more sensible from now on. We'll sell all this and buy you a crib or something a little more useful." I say stroking my stomach.

I snap pictures of each item before boxing or wrapping them back up and moving onto the next. By the time I'm done, my camera roll is full of my beautiful shoes, handbags, and clothes and my back aches from the awkward position I was sitting in.

Standing, I go to stretch out my sore muscles when movement by the door catches my eye.

"Holy shit, Brandon. You scared the crap out of me."

"Sorry," he says, his cheeks brightening a little.

"Were you watching me?"

"I'm still a little gobsmacked by how much stuff you have."

"You carried it all in here, you should be more than aware." I try to laugh it off but the way he's looking at me right now has a weird knot twisting my stomach and an ache in my chest I don't think I've experienced before.

He's standing in a pair of grey sweatpants and a white t-shirt. It's simple and not the kind of thing I've ever found particularly sexy on a man, but right this second it's all I can do to stand here panting with need.

My eyes zero in on the slight bulge behind the fabric and images of him giving me what I needed the other night fill my mind.

I was inconsolable when I laid on my bed that night as I tried to accept my fate, but the second I opened the door to him, everything just got that little bit better. I've no idea what happened to the other woman, and in that moment I didn't really care because more than anything, I needed to be in his arms.

When I'd told him what I'd needed he didn't even bat an eyelid in stripping off and giving it to me. I'd expected him to fuck me, to give me exactly what my body was craving and to get the hell out, but that was the opposite of what I got. Because the reality was much more gentle and passionate.

"Are you okay? Do you feel all right?"

"Yeah, yeah," I say, shaking the thoughts from my head. "Just trying to get my head around selling all this lot."

"Take your time; we've still a few months before we really need this room." He seems all too happy about me continuing to occupy his bed. I can't help feeling like I'm holding him back. He was clearly dating before. I really shouldn't be getting in the way.

"I'd rather just get it sorted as soon as possible."

"Okay, well, if you need any help, I'll be out in the garage. I've got a coffee table to finish off."

"Okay," I whisper, emotion burning at my throat.

"What?"

"It's nothing. I'm just being silly." He raises an eyebrow for me to tell him anyway and after sucking in a big breath of courage I do. "I don't want to do this alone," I confess. "What are you doing?" I ask, when he kicks his shoes off and walks into the room.

"Keeping you company."

"But... But you've got a coffee table to—"

"I'll do it later. I can't bear the look on your face right now."

"What look?"

"The one that tells me you'll burst into tears if I walk away." His eyes soften and the tears he's talking about pool in my eyes at his thoughtfulness.

"No, I wasn't," I argue. His head tilts to the side and a smile twitches his lips.

"Where do you want me?"

My eyes drop down his body. *Naked and laid on the floor waiting for me to ride you,* I think, but I manage to keep my thoughts to myself. When I find Brandon's eyes once again, I swear there's fire burning within them.

Neither of us acts on the tension crackling between us as I get back to work.

"You done in here now?"

I nod.

"Come on then, I'll make us a drink."

He starts the coffee machine while I sit myself

at the table and start writing up descriptions for everything I've photographed.

"I dread to think how much that lot must have cost you," he muses as he crashes about in the kitchen.

"I'd rather not think about it right now. It would probably keep a roof over my head for longer than I want to admit."

"You don't need to worry about that now, Reese. You're more than welcome to stay here for as long as you need."

"Why are you being so nice to me? I've been nothing but a complete bitch to you most of the time."

"You're growing our baby, cupcake. It's the least I can do." I open my mouth to respond but no words come out. Because I like him being nice to me and I'm not ready to face up to why that might be yet. "Are you okay now if I..." He trails off, nodding down towards his garage.

"Yeah, thank you. I'll make some lunch soon and bring it down for you."

"I didn't think you could cook?"

"I'm not sure fixing a sandwich constitutes as cooking."

"Hmm, I'm going to need to teach you before bean arrives."

"You've never struck me as the domesticated type either, Brandon." I arch a brow at him.

"I can cook. I just got myself in a rut where I couldn't be bothered with anything. Cooking, cleaning, life, really. But I can actually cook quite well and I'll give you a few lessons if you like."

"We'll see," I mutter, feeling inadequate to become a mother but afraid of allowing him to see it.

"Don't worry, cupcake. I've got you. There's nothing to worry about." As if he can sense exactly how I'm feeling and what I need, he walks over, threads his fingers through my hair and drops his lips to my forehead. His heat settles whatever it was inside me that was starting to panic. It feels… nice, that is until he stands back and leaves the room. Then I'm just alone and cold once again.

I list a few items before my stomach starts rumbling. So placing my phone down on the table, I head over to see what I can knock up for lunch.

His fridge is full of fresh ingredients. It reminds me of my mother's and has a shiver of terror running down my spine.

Ignoring some of the more obscure items, I

reach for a tub of butter and cheese. I can't go wrong with a cheese sandwich, right?

I eventually find the bread and sigh in frustration when I don't find it already sliced. I grab a knife and attempt to cut off what I need.

With two plates of questionable looking sandwiches in my hands, I manage to balance them while I open the back door and head down to Brandon.

Music sounds out long before I get to the door and I can't help the beat perking me up a little.

Pushing the door open, I peer inside. My eyes run over a few stunning pieces of furniture that he's ready to ship to their new home and I'm shown once again just how wrong I was about him. I thought he was a lazy arse with a bullshit job. I had no idea that he was capable of something as incredible as this. I feel a little sick as I think about the fact I probably would have treated him differently if I'd known he could do this. He was right. I really was a judgemental arsehole.

A grunt makes me take another step into the garage. I look up and my eyes widen. Brandon's standing over a stunning looking coffee table. His shirt's off and his skin is covered in a sheen of sweat as he lovingly sands the top of the table.

I've no idea how long I stand there staring as his muscles ripple and flex, but I do know that by the time he realises he has company and looks up at me, I'm about three seconds from stripping my clothes off and demanding he takes me on the damn table.

No wonder he's so good with his hands...

"Oh, hey. I didn't hear you come in. I'm starved. What did you make?"

"It's... uh... it's a sex—" *Fuck my life.* "A *cheese* sandwich."

"Jesus, Reese. What did you cut the bread with, my saw?" My cheeks heat and a sick feeling settles in my belly. I fucking hate feeling inadequate. "It's perfect, Reese. I'm only winding you up." I know he's only trying to make me feel better. I have eyes, I can see what a car crash my sandwiches are.

"So..." I start, looking around his garage, trying to distract myself from his still shirtless body. "Sweaty work that coffee table, huh?"

"Oh, shit. Sorry." Putting his plate down, he drags his shirt over his head and covers up, making me regret saying anything. "Better?"

I mumble some kind of agreement and attempt to get my doorstop of a sandwich into my mouth.

The silence gets a little awkward between us. Every movement and noise he makes has me on the edge of suggesting we do something stupid. That is until his phone lights up on his workbench.

Lauren: Fancy hooking up tonight?

WE BOTH STARE down at the little preview. Dread sits heavy in my stomach, but I can't help thinking that this is a sign. A sign that I shouldn't be getting too comfortable here. Or getting too used to having Brandon to lean on.

"You should go. On the date I mean."

"I should? I thought we were going to be friends with benefits?"

"I've changed my mind. That would complicate things. Anyway, you don't want to be stuck here, with me in my pyjamas with a tub of ice cream. You should still be able to go out and have some fun."

"But—"

"Yeah. I think it would be better all round if we just stay friends, with no other complications. It'd be better for our co-parenting future." I lie, all but running from the garage.

Brandon calls out for me, but I don't stop. This thing between us is starting to freak me out. I know I just told him to agree to his hook up later, but really, it's the last thing I want. I'd much rather he was with me on the sofa as we watched a movie together. And there lies the problem. He's my brother's best friend. He's supposed to be JUST my baby daddy. Anything else is too complicated.

I lock myself in the spare room claiming that I'm still going through all my stuff when he eventually comes in from the garage and starts getting ready for his night out.

"Are you sure you're all right with me going out?"

"I'm more than all right, I'm looking forward to an evening to myself. A relax. You need me to help you choose an outfit or anything?"

He stares at me for a few seconds as if he's waiting for me to confess that I'm lying, before saying he's fine and heading towards the bathroom.

I focus on what I'm doing and don't allow any other thoughts to enter my head until I hear the front door shut behind him. It's only then I allow myself to surrender to the emotions running rampant around my body.

It's right that he's out with someone else. It's how it needs to be. The thought of the two of us being together is laughable at best. We're polar opposites and he's everything I always said I never wanted. *So why do you want him more than anyone you've ever met?*

Fed up of talking myself in circles, I grab my phone and pull up Sarah's name.

"Hey, how's the baby?"

"Good. Growing nicely and thankfully making me throw up less."

"And how's the daddy?"

"I moved in with him," I blurt.

"Fuck. I thought you hated him?"

"So did I, but..."

"But..." she encourages.

"I lost my job and can't afford to stay in my place. He offered for me to move in."

"Wow."

"And now he's out on a date that I made him go on and I kind of hate myself," I admit in a rush, just needing to get the words out of my mouth.

"Wow," she repeats, making me fall down onto

the sofa and drop my head into my hands. What the hell am I doing right now?

"So let me get this straight. You moved in with the baby daddy who you described to me as a hobo? Reese 'immaculate' Connors is living with the great unwashed and untidy?"

"He cleaned up his act. Big time."

"What aren't you telling me, Reese?"

"I think I might be having feelings for the hobo, but then again it could just be my hormones. I'm a mess, Sarah, and I don't know what to do."

"Well, maybe encouraging him to date someone else wasn't your best move," she suggests.

"I know." I sigh. "Tell me about what's going on in your world right now. I need distracting." I urge and I curl up on the sofa while I hear about life in the Lake District.

13

BRANDON

I DON'T KNOW what to do.

There's no way I want to hook up with another woman tonight, but Reese wouldn't take no for an answer. Maybe it's hormones, or maybe she's freaking out. It seemed easier for me to agree to go out in the end, so I pretended to go on a date. In reality, I actually called my old housemate, Aiden, and asked him to meet me for a beer.

"Missing me, mate?" he announces loudly as he walks towards me. I'm sat at a table nursing a pint and I'm sure I look as fed up as I feel.

"Life was a lot less fucking complicated when I lived with you." I take another sip.

"Jesus, who died?"

"No one. Just got a lot on my plate and I know

it's not really a man thing, but I actually do need to talk to someone."

"Isn't Jack free?"

"Jack's not all that keen on me right now."

"Oh?"

I sighed.

"I may have got his sister pregnant."

There's a stunned silence. "You could have waited until I'd got myself a pint and a seat. Fucking hell, Brandon. Sit tight. I'll get you another pint while I'm there."

The pub's half full. Enough for my conversation to be lost amongst the hum of the rest of the patrons. Aiden would normally sit opposite me but on this occasion takes the stool at the side of me instead.

"Start from the beginning and tell me everything."

"Everything?"

"Well, without intimate details of your, shall we call it, *dalliances* with Jack's sister."

"You have to promise not to breathe a word about any of this because I've not got my own head around what's going on in my brain yet. I just feel like I need to talk it out with someone."

"Okay. Scout's honour."

I tell him about how we got together at the wedding. How Reese was pregnant. That she'd lost her job and had moved in. How we'd told Jack and his parents that we were dating and seeing how things went.

"Okay, well that all seems perfectly reasonable and sensible."

I sigh. "Yes, except I think I might be developing feelings for her and I don't want them."

He looks down his nose at me. "You're speaking of love like it's some kind of fungus, Brandon."

Mention of the L-word almost causes me to have a full-blown panic attack. I gulp down the remainder of my first pint and make a dint in the second.

"Now steady on, Brandon. Come on, mate, I've never seen you like this. What's going on?"

"That's just it. I don't know. I'm overwhelmed by everything. I'm going to be a dad. That's one thing. I have this new career that's exploding. That's another. I'm trying to keep up with all this appearance and clean house thing, and now I have a woman living in my home who is encouraging me to date while carrying my baby."

"Oh." Aiden's face falls. "She's encouraging you to date?"

"Yes. So picture this. The woman pregnant with your baby wants you to give her sex whenever she's rampant for it, but she also wants you to date other women."

"Mate, that's what most men's fantasies are made of."

"Yes, well the reality is a lot different. My life was so much easier when I went to work, came home and fell asleep on the sofa."

"Except that wasn't life. It was like a living death. I was worried for you, mate."

I mull over his words for a minute or two.

"I need you to come out with me for drinks or let me go around yours while I'm supposed to be on dates with other women. Just for now, until I can work out what I want. The last thing I need to be doing is dating other women, my life is complicated enough."

"You're insane. Just go and tell her about everything that's going on with you."

"No. She just lost her job, had to move into a strange home, and is pregnant. She's enough on her mind without my confused feelings."

Aiden sighs. "I'll do it for a month. Then you need to have talked to her or calmed yourself down."

"Thanks, pal. Another pint?"

"Yes, and this time we can use it to celebrate the fact that you're not the only one set to be a father."

My eyes widen. "Kaylie is pregnant?"

He nods, but where my expression is one of confusion, he beams with happiness. And therein lies the difference in our situations. Aiden is settled and in love.

"Almost four months. We've only told close family so far."

I get up to go to the bar and grab my friend in a bear hug. "Congrats, dude."

"Likewise."

I RETURN WITH OUR PINTS, sit down, and blow out a huge breath.

"I'm going to be a part-time single dad. It's only a few months ago I could barely look after myself and now I'll be responsible for a baby."

"Hey, if it doesn't work out with Reese, think of

the benefits. You'll be a hot single dad. One of those who walks around the place with his cute baby in a papoose with all the women drooling right along with the baby."

There definitely is something wrong with me because this doesn't excite me at all.

"What happened with Naomi…"

I take a sharp intake of breath.

"You were so young, Brandon. You can't let that define your future."

"I made her my whole world." I stare into space. "There was no one but her, and then I found out it was all lies on her part. She never loved me at all. I was the nice guy her father wanted for her, when she was in love with someone else all along."

"And she's no doubt got on with her life. She's probably married with kids and you're what? Letting her still affect you now? That's some power you've given her."

"The hurt was excruciating."

"Look, Brandon. How long did it take me and Kaylie to get together? We're so happy but we can't help but regret all those years we maybe could have been more. Don't waste any more of your life. Start living it."

We spend the rest of the evening chatting sports, but my head is still thinking about Reese.

On my way home I call in at the 24-hour supermarket and spray myself with a woman's body spray. I pick the lipstick tester off the display and smudge a bit on my collar. There we go. Proof of a date.

I walk into the house but it's quiet and the upstairs lights are off. Discarding my own clothes, I make my way upstairs and into my bedroom. Reese is asleep on the bed and the moonlight from the window lights up her face enough for me to be able to see how peaceful she looks right now.

I climb in at the side of her and watch her for a moment, wondering if I should pull her into my arms. Then as my eyes start to close while my mind wars with itself, I turn over to face the other way and fall asleep.

April

ANOTHER MONTH HAS PASSED. Reese thinks I've continued to date and she hasn't asked me for sex once. I have blue balls. She's taken to selling shoes and bags like a duck to water and now she's feeling better and less sick she's running it as a small business, buying and selling pieces online and even going out to charity shops some days. She's like a different woman to the Ice Queen I knew. That tautness about her has gone. She's relaxed. I even left a glass out yesterday and she didn't move it. Today is the day of our meal at the house. Jack and Rhian are coming. Me and Jack have been talking tentatively of late via text messages, but we've not been out for a pint or anything. Today we're showing them how well our dating and living together is going. In other words, we're about to lie.

The table is set. The house is clean and tidy and between us we've cooked a Sunday lunch. To ensure Jack doesn't stab me with a carving knife, we also invited Aiden and Kaylie. Safety in numbers and all that.

Reese comes downstairs from getting changed and she's dressed in a black knitted dress with leggings. It shows off the slight curve of her pregnant belly and the swell of those tits that are blossoming as she is. I want to part her legs and fuck her over the table.

"You look amazing."

"Do you think you can tell I'm pregnant yet?"

"A little, I think." I walk over to her. "Can I?"

She nods.

I run my hand over the swell of her stomach. "Hey there, bean."

We're standing so close together; so close that I hear her breath hitch as I touch her.

And the doorbell goes and shatters the moment. Reese jumps back. "I'll answer it."

"Sure thing, cupcake." I wink at her.

Aiden and Kaylie come in and I don't miss Reese looking at Kaylie's more rounded stomach. They start chatting babies, while Aiden comes towards me and starts helping put out glasses, seeing as they're still in the same place as when he lived here.

"There's water, wine, beer, cordial," I tell him. "Help yourself."

"You can have a beer. I'll drive back." Kaylie shouts over at him.

"You can have a beer too, snookums." Reese blows me a kiss.

Aiden sniggers. "Snookums?"

I lower my voice. "It's part of the acting like a

couple in front of Jack thing. We've developed pet names for each other."

"Well, don't worry. Kaylie won't say anything."

"You told her?" I feel the panic hit my system.

"We don't have secrets. But don't worry, she'll keep your secrets. She promised me."

The doorbell rings again and this time it's Jack and Rhian at the door.

Finally, everyone is sitting at the dinner table. Jack is being more like his old self with me, although there's still an awkwardness between us. As Reese and I serve dinner we cuddle, call each other pet names and tap each other's bottoms.

"Have you ever seen three couples so loved up?" Aiden asks as we eat. "Who'd have thought we'd all be here like this, when not long ago there was only Jack dating."

I join in. "It's unbelievable to think that I was a slobby mess, who'd practically given up on life, and thanks to you and Jack who encouraged my makeover, now I'm in love and going to be a dad." I smile over at Reese. "Thank you for making my life complete, cupcake."

"Yes," Reese smiles back. "I know you've been super-protective of me, Jack, like I'd expect of my big brother, but you were the one who showed me who Brandon really was. I had no idea of the hottie hiding away under those lazy layers, and the kind man hiding under those protective ones."

I continue back. "And I hadn't realised that under the woman I'd dubbed Ice Queen there was actually a beautiful woman inside and out who was also hiding under her own protective layers. I couldn't think of anyone more perfect to be my baby mama, and I'm so excited for the future."

Reese's eyes mist up and I watch her wipe under them. Jack clears his throat. "I'd like to say something."

Fuck.

"When I first found out my sister was pregnant and you were the father, I wasn't exactly happy about things."

Understatement of the year.

"I admit it's taken me some time to get used to the idea, because you're my best mate, and you're my little sister and Reese, I don't think I'd have been happy about anybody knocking you up, cos big brother and all that, but..." He looks from one of us to the other. "I can see how happy you are making each other. It's clear you have something special, and I, well, I want to say I'm happy for you and I can't wait to be an uncle."

I do believe my best mate has a tear in his eye and then so does Reese and they are up and hugging and I feel all mixed up again, because I'm either the biggest shit in the world for lying to him or the biggest idiot in the world for lying to myself.

But which one is it?

14

REESE

RHIAN AND JACK excuse themselves and leave not long after, leaving just Brandon, Aiden, Kaylie and I sitting around the table.

I'd been dreading this evening, but I've been pleasantly surprised by how much I've actually enjoyed it. I had no idea if Jack was going to come around to the idea of Brandon and I, not that there really is an us, but he seemed pretty happy about the fact we're having a baby together. He even seemed genuinely excited about becoming an uncle.

Things with Brandon have been weird over the past few weeks. I've tried to keep myself busy, setting up my new online second-hand store and visiting charity stores to find my stock, but it's not stopped me freaking out about our situation or stopped my eyes wandering whenever he's in the room.

The longer I'm here, the stronger the pull I feel towards him gets. And that is dangerous, especially because he's out dating, just like I insisted he did. He's been out at least twice a week, forcing me to sit around and watch as he gets himself ready to spend the evening and maybe longer with another woman. The jealousy is starting to eat me alive; not that I'd ever let on.

Lying beside him every night is torture. I so desperately want to feel the weight of his arms around me, his soft lips against my shoulder, his cock as he... "No," I say aloud, not meaning to. All heads turn towards me, eyes wide, waiting for me to explain why I just interrupted them.

"I'm sorry," I mutter. "Why don't you all take this into the living room?"

"Sounds good, another beer?" Brandon asks Aiden before getting up and going to the fridge. Unlike all the other times when we were pretending in front of Jack, he doesn't lean down to press a kiss to my temple or run a hand over my shoulder lovingly and I miss it.

I keep my head down, tears pooling at the

corners of my eyes as he grabs a couple of bottles and heads towards the living room. Aiden goes to follow and Kaylie pushes her chair out but I feel her stare. It's the main reason I refuse to look up. While everyone has happily accepted the two of us are embarking on a new life as a couple, Kaylie's eyes have been assessing me, digging deeper and I don't like the idea of what she might find.

"I'll join you in a bit. I just need to use the toilet, again," she sighs, making me smile as she walks from the room with her hand on her belly. She is absolutely glowing and I'm envious. I just feel like a lump right now. None of my clothes fit, yet I haven't got the cute bump she has to show why. I just feel... totally unsexy. It's no wonder Brandon is out getting what he can elsewhere.

With them all gone, I make myself busy clearing away the mess. I'm happier hiding in here doing my thing than continuing trying to fake this thing between us. It's draining both mentally and physically and I'm about ready to fall face first into bed. *A bed that smells like him and will only remind you of what you want and don't have.*

Shaking away my inner critic, I scrape the plates and stack them ready for washing.

"I feel like I spend most of my life in the toilets

these days," Kaylie moans when she comes back in and slows to a stop next to me.

"W- what are you doing?" I ask when she grabs a towel and sets to work.

"Helping. I don't really need to be in there listening to another conversation about football."

"You don't need to help. You're our guest."

"It's really okay. Plus, I thought it would give us time to talk; to get to know each other better without the boys."

As much as I don't want a heart to heart with the woman who's spent all night trying to put the pieces together in her head, the prospect of talking to another pregnant woman who might have all the same fears I do is tempting.

"As long as you're sure."

"So how are you finding things, morning sickness worn off now?"

We chat away about bumps, and thankfully she steers away from any more probing questions. I find that I actually quite like her company. With Sarah being so far away and Rhian embarking on her new married life, I hadn't realised how much I'd missed girl time.

"Would you like a hot drink? We've got decaf coffee, tea of most varieties, hot chocolate?"

"Oh, do you have cream and marshmallows?"

"We do," I say with a wide smile thinking about my craving a few weeks ago.

"What's that look for?"

"Brandon went out at midnight to get it all a week or so back because I craved a hot chocolate. He brought back the works."

"Aw, that's so sweet. He's really doting on you, huh?"

"He's just excited about the baby."

She lets the conversation hang while I prepare the mugs of goodness and find a seat with her at the table.

"Here you go."

"Thank you."

"I think he's more than excited about the baby, Reese. I've never seen him as happy as he is right now."

I shrug, a lump of emotion crawling up my throat. "He's going to be a great dad."

"I've no doubt. But what about everything else?"

"What do you mean?"

"Don't you think he'd be a good boyfriend... or husband maybe, one day?"

"I... uh... He's dating other women. This thing

between us, it's an act for my family." Tears pool in my eyes at admitting the truth. My chest constricts like someone's tied an elastic band around it.

"I know," Kaylie says softly, reaching her hand out to squeeze mine. "Only, that's not quite true, Reese."

My eyes fly up to meet hers. "It's not?"

Shaking her head, she sips her drink and moans in pleasure. She glances over to the doorway to make sure we don't have company. "I shouldn't be telling you this, but... when he's been telling you he's out dating, he's... he's actually with Aiden or at our house."

"He's what? Why?" Confused, my brows draw together but it's my heart that starts to get carried away with itself as it thunders in my chest.

"Because it's what you told him you wanted."

"What I—fuck."

"You told him to date, to meet other woman, and see if he could find the one. But as far as he's concerned, I'm pretty sure he thinks he's found her."

"But—" My chest heaves as I fight to catch my breath. "He comes in smelling of other women."

"I caught him spraying himself with my body spray, Reese. He's trying to do what you want, to be what you need. But seeing you both tonight, it's pretty clear that what you need and want is him."

"I—" Her eyes soften as she stares at me.

"Trust me, I know how hard this is. I was terrified of things changing between Aiden and me, but it was the best thing I've ever done. If you want him, you deserve to see where it could take you."

I'm silent for a few seconds as her words spin around in my head. "I've never been in a real relationship," I admit quietly.

"So? I don't think he cares how experienced you are at all this. You're carrying his baby and he wants the real deal, Reese. The question is, do you?"

Do I?

Nothing more is said between us and thankfully Aiden comes in to ensure that's the end of it.

"You ready to make a move, babe?"

"Yep. Let me just wee again."

Aiden chuckles softly and his eyes follow Kaylie from the room, love and adoration pouring from them. I want a man to look at me like that.

Aiden makes small talk, but I can tell he's holding himself back.

Once Kaylie rejoins us, I thank them for

coming and Kaylie and I briefly arrange to meet for some baby talk in a few weeks before they disappear to say goodbye to Brandon, who seems to be hiding in the living room.

It's only a few minutes later when the front door shuts and the house falls silent. My heart pounds in my chest knowing he's only feet away and that his secret has just been revealed. But what should I do about it?

Do I continue as we were in an attempt to protect my heart, or act on what I want and see where it takes us?

Wasting a little more time, I make myself another drink and grab the packet of biscuits from the cupboard.

The second I step through into the living room, his eyes turn to me.

"Hey."

"Hey. You feeling okay?"

"Yeah. Brandon?" His eyebrows lift for me to continue. "How was your date last night?"

His mouth opens, but no words come out for a few seconds. "It- it was good."

"Really? You were home pretty early."

"Yeah well. I wasn't really up for it."

"Right. Something to do with the date being a guy maybe?"

All the colour drains from his face.

"Goes by the name of Aiden, maybe?"

"How'd you...? Fuck. Kaylie."

"Yeah, Kaylie. Why have you been lying to me, Brandon?"

The tension crackles between us as I wait for his response. He twists the bottle in his hands and chews down on his lip.

"It's... fuck." Standing, he shoves his hand deep in his pocket, refusing to meet my eyes. "It's what you said you wanted."

"Yeah, because I thought it was what you wanted." It's only half true because my biggest concern was allowing myself to fall for him, but I fear it's now too late for that.

"I never wanted anyone else, Reese."

He takes a step forward and finds my eyes. My heart races and my hands tremble. He must sense it because when he's close enough, he reaches out and takes the mug from my hand, dropping it to the coffee table.

"Reese," he breathes, his palm cupping my cheek as he stares deep in my eyes. "I haven't so much as looked at another woman since you moved in."

"But the lipstick on your collar..." I thought it was a little cliché at the time but pushed it aside.

"I put it there," he confesses.

15

———

BRANDON

"I SPRAYED PERFUME ON MYSELF, either supermarket deodorant sprays or Kaylie's. I put lipstick on my collars, so you'd think I went out. See, I thought it was what you wanted; you kept asking me to date other women. Tell me what you want, Reese. I need to be clear before I make another move."

"I don't want you to date other women," she says and my heart starts to beat in anticipation that she might actually feel the same way.

"I'm not, so that's sorted. What else?"

"I want you. Take me to bed, Brandon."

That's not enough for me. I need her to tell me how she feels.

"Is that all you want from me, Reese? A fuck

buddy?"

She shakes her head and once again those vulnerable eyes look up to mine. "No. I want you, Brandon. I want all of you. I- I think I'm falling in love with you."

I sweep her into my arms and get ready to carry her up the stairs where I can put claim to her. She's mine. All mine.

And then the doorbell goes.

"Ignore it," I whisper into her ear, my mouth on her neck.

"I can't. I totally forgot. It's a woman coming to pick up a load of clothes and shoes she bought from me. She's come all the way from Manchester."

I put her down at the bottom of the stairs.

We look at each other and start laughing.

"I hope she's not here long," I groan.

But of course she is. The woman insists on trying everything on, having a drink, and basically telling Reese all about her life, while I hover on the periphery making sure she's not a female serial killer.

Waiting for her to leave is the longest wait of my life.

Because what happens when she goes could change everything.

THINGS WITH BRANDON are just about to explode, along with my libido, and then the door goes. It's almost two hours later when the woman eventually hands over a stack of cash and I'm forced to say goodbye to some of my much-loved shoes and bags. I fight down the emotion that threatens to clog my throat. I know they're just things and that it's ridiculous to get so attached to them. But I worked my arse off and those things were my reward. It wasn't like I had much else in my life to celebrate my success with.

I let out a huge sigh when I eventually close the front door behind her. Tears burn at the back of my throat and my teeth sink into my bottom lip in the hope it'll stop it trembling.

I'm just about to turn when I feel his presence behind me. The air surrounding me vanishes and I fight to drag in the air I need knowing I'm under his stare.

He's been standing in the corner watching me for the past two hours, ensuring that the tingles he caused in me earlier didn't abate even a tiny bit. If I thought I wanted him earlier when he was about to carry me up to his bed, then it's nothing compared to how much I want him right now.

I keep my eyes downcast, afraid that he'll see too much if I look at him. I need to get myself under control before going to him. But I don't get the chance because as I go to step forward, he beats me to it. The warmth of his hand wraps around the back of my neck and his lips find my forehead.

"Reese?" His voice is so soft, it does nothing for my raging emotions. With the fingers of his other hand, he tilts my head up so I've no choice but to look at him.

His breath catches when his eyes find mine. "Reese, baby. What's wrong?"

I shake my head, afraid that if I open my mouth a sob will fall out. Everything just feels too much right now. Our confessions before the knock on the door, selling all my old stuff. My head starts to feel a little fuzzy and my heart races.

"You still want me?"

I hate that I've made him question what I said before.

"Yes, Brandon. Yes."

"You... sure?"

Not bothering with words, I reach up on my tiptoes and press my lips to his. Actions speak louder than words anyway, right?

His hands skim around my waist before coming to a stop on my arse. I jump when he goes to lift me and my legs wrap around his waist, desperate to feel more of him.

My back presses into the hallway wall as he kisses me deeper. It's different to any of our kisses before. It's not rushed and full of lust. It's thoughtful, each slow movement considered, and it's full of emotion. He's telling me everything he's been keeping inside all these weeks through his kiss.

A moan rumbles up my throat when he rocks his hips into me.

"Shit, Brandon."

"You've no idea how long I've been dreaming

about this," he mutters against the soft skin of my neck as he trails his lips down to my collarbone.

"I- I think I do. Fuck, I need you."

"I so badly want to take you right here."

"So do it."

"One day. Right now, you deserve more than that."

He pulls me from the wall and with his lips still connected to my neck, he effortlessly carries me up the stairs and deposits me on his bed.

I sit back on my palms as he reaches over his head and pulls his polo shirt off. My eyes feast on the inches of skin he reveals. My mouth waters to lick the lines of his abs.

Next, his hands drop to his waistband, and his jeans and boxers drop to the floor. He's fully hard already, the sight making my muscles clench in preparation for feeling him sliding inside me.

Stalking over to me, he bends slightly so he can capture my lips in a knee-weakening kiss.

"Lift up," he mumbles as his fingers grip the bottom of my dress and pull upwards. Our lips only part long enough for the fabric to pass and then he's back on me.

My bra is removed and thrown over his

shoulder before he crawls over me, making me lie back.

He finds one of my nipples and pinches and pulls gently while I whimper and mewl. Skimming his hands down my side, he tucks his fingers inside my leggings and knickers and pulls them down. His lips follow their descent, sucking each nipple into his mouth and kissing down over my rounded stomach.

"I hope you're asleep in there. You don't need to witness what I'm about to do to your mummy." I want to laugh at the ridiculousness of this situation but the conviction behind his words as he talks to our baby is too endearing and I once again find myself tearing up.

"I'm sorry. I—"

"Don't you dare apologise for that." Threading my fingers into his hair, I force him to look up at me. The confession I made downstairs before we were interrupted slams into me and with his soft eyes staring up at me, I can't help feeling even more like they were true. I really am falling in love with Brandon Weston and there's fuck all I can do about it.

Is he the kind of man I pictured I'd spend my life with? No.

Is the life we're building together one I pictured for my future? No.

But is it everything I want? Yes. Yes, I think it is.

"I love you, Brandon."

"Fuck." He almost looks like the words that just left my mouth were painful to hear, that is until his lips curl up into a smile. "I think I love you too, Ice Queen." He winks before continuing with his final descent and settling between my legs. "I'm sorry, bean," he whispers before parting me and circling my clit with the tip of his tongue.

"Oh God," I moan when he also slips a finger inside me. This has been a long time coming and I can already feel my impending orgasm building.

He presses deeper, bending his fingers in a way that has my back arching and my toes curling.

"Brandon, I'm— Brandon," I squeal as my orgasm slams into me. At no point does he stop. His tongue continues licking and his fingers thrusting inside me until he's drawn out every drop of pleasure my release can give me. "Fuck." My heart races, my nerves tingling as Brandon climbs back up to capture my lips. Tasting myself on him only ensures the aftershocks of my orgasm continue. He kisses me like he wants to devour me, his tongue duelling with mine, our teeth clashing as he lines himself up with my entrance.

He grunts and sit back as he fills me to the hilt. The muscles in his neck and shoulder strain as he tries to keep himself in check.

"Let go, Brandon. Give me everything you're trying to hold back."

"Fuck, you're perfect."

I go to respond but I don't get a chance because he hits me so deep that all I can do is focus on the feeling and give myself over to him completely.

His thrusts get harder and harder. Sweat beads his brow and he continues whispering about how much he needs me. Sex has never been like this. I've only ever felt like it was an act to get pleasure; never this intimate, emotion-filled experience that has tears stinging my eyes and my heart threatening to beat right out of my damn chest.

Totally spent, Brandon falls to his side, pulling me close to him. "That was... wow."

"This is crazy." I don't mean for my thoughts to come out aloud and I hate myself the second I feel him tense beside me.

"Don't you want this?" The panic in his voice has me lifting myself up so I can see him properly.

"That wasn't meant to sound like a bad thing."

Placing my hand on his chest, I delight that my simple touch causes his eyelids to flicker. "I just meant that here we are living together, having a baby, exchanging I love you's and we've not even had a date."

His brows draw together. "You want a date?"

"No, that wasn't me going a long way around asking you to take me out. I was just saying, it's crazy."

"It's most definitely crazy. A few months ago, I thought I hated you; now look at us."

I try to look offended by his comment, but I can't. It seems he really has softened my ice-cold heart. "That feeling was entirely mutual, slob."

He's silent for a few minutes lost in his thoughts. I fall back to the bed and allow him the time he needs.

"Friday night. Get dressed up. I'll pick you up at eight."

"Brandon, I really didn't—"

"Shhh... I know, but now you've mentioned it, I can't think of anything other than going out with you on my arm and showing you off as mine."

His words cause heat to spread through my body. "That's the only thing you can think about right now?" I trail my fingers over his chest and abs, his cock twitching and swelling at my touch.

"You're naked and in my bed, dinner most certainly isn't the only thing I'm thinking about."

"Good because we've got a lot of time to waste between now and Friday."

I squeal and laugh as he pulls me on top of him. "Come on then, Miss Control Freak. Show me how it's done."

17

BRANDON

I'M RUNNING a little behind with my furniture orders.

Because I've been taking bedroom orders from Reese instead.

This morning I've left her catching up on some much-needed sleep while I get myself caught up a little. Tonight is our date night. I've booked InHale, which is a really swanky London restaurant owned by Kaylie's brother Jenson. I made sure to ask for a romantic corner table.

I feel nervous, which is ridiculous given I'm taking out the woman I'm living with.

After getting ready that evening, I excuse myself from the house saying I need to go get something and I'll be back to pick her up at eight.

While I'm out I go to a florist and pick up a massive bouquet of flowers. Exiting the car on my return, I ring my own doorbell.

Keese opens the door and her eyes widen. "I wondered who it could be at this time. You daft sod ringing the doorbell."

I produce the flowers from behind my back.

"These are for you."

She puts a hand over her heart. "Wow. For me? How very romantic Mr Weston. Would you like to come in?"

"How very forward of you, Miss Connors. Maybe later, but for now I would very much like to take you out on a date. Would you like to come and eat dinner with me?"

"I would. Just allow me to put the flowers in the sink in some water and I'll be ready."

After waiting for her to sort out the flowers, I think about how gorgeous she looks. When she returns I tell her.

"That dress looks beautiful on you."

She looks down at the red wrap dress that accentuates her curves.

"Thank you."

"You look sexy as fuck. I can't wait to peel it off you later."

She nudges my arm. "Stop or we'll never get there."

I park in the staff car park of InHale, a favour arranged via Kaylie, and we walk inside. I take in the shiny black floors, mirrored walls, and square and rectangular dining tables with red tablecloths. I feel a little out of my depth; I've never frequented anywhere this fancy before. This restaurant has won awards!

The waiter comes over to escort us to our seat. I see his name badge says Scott. He's a good-looking guy and I see him look Reese up and down appraisingly.

"Is the baby okay?" I blurt out at her.

Reese looks at me strangely. "Yes, why wouldn't it be?"

I shrug as we follow Scott to our table. "I just wondered if the food smells might affect it. Like if you get really hungry it gets jumpy or something." Great start to our date night, me talking absolute crap. At least Scott's interest seems to have waned now.

He goes to pull out Reese's chair, but I stop him. "If I could do that please?"

"Of course, Sir. I will just get you the drinks menu."

When he comes back, he opens the drinks menu and hands it to Reese. "Here are the soft drinks. There are also virgin cocktails, as in no alcohol, obviously." He winks.

Reese giggles. "Yes, I wouldn't be able to have it otherwise. I think it's pretty obvious I'm not one of those."

"So when are you due?"

"I'd like a coke please." I interrupt. "Do you know what you want to drink, darling?"

A smirk hovers over Reese's mouth. "Well, snookums, I'm just deciding."

Another member of staff with short spiky dark hair comes over. She nods and pulls the guy to one side but I can hear the venom in her voice. "What's taking so long, Scott? We're busy. Do you have the drinks order yet?"

"Were you missing me, babes?"

"Yes, I keep throwing the knives but obviously need more practice. Now the drinks order?"

"I haven't been able to get it yet because you interrupted."

"Scott! Oh my god, you're impossible." She stomps off.

Scott walks back over. "Sorry about that. She's been given several warnings about her attitude already. I'd better take your order before she stomps back over."

Reese orders a non-alcoholic mojito and Scott moves on.

"That's a bit of a dramatic start to our date, don't you think?" Reese says, her eyes looking over at where Scott has taken the drinks order to the female bartender who is clearly shouting at him.

"Well he was dawdling."

"Their sexual chemistry is off the charts hot. If they aren't banging, they should be."

"Reese! Anyway, I don't agree. She clearly hates him."

Reese shakes her head at me. "There's no wonder you've been single for so long."

The bartender walks over with our drinks and sets them down. Her name badge says Suki. "My apologies for earlier. Just a small disagreement between us. It wasn't professional and I really am terribly sorry if you heard any of our conversation."

"I found it quite entertaining," Reese says. "What's the story between you two, if you don't mind me asking? Is he an ex?"

Suki's brow creases. "God, no. Eww. I wouldn't touch him with a bargepole. He's hideous, and probably sexually diseased." She places a hand over her mouth. "Oh my god, I am so sorry again. He's going to be the reason I lose my job here."

She goes rushing off to serve other customers and Reese smiles at me. "I'm a lawyer. I can spot lies a mile off. They are so hot for each other, even if neither of them will admit it."

"I really don't see it."

"There's a fine line between love and hate, remember?"

I wink at her. "Ice Queen."

She winks back. "Slob."

I lean forward and run a hand up her thigh. "Cupcake."

She runs her tongue around her top lip. "Snookums."

THE MEAL IS divine and we chat just like people would on a date. Not a first date, although that's what this is, because over the last few weeks we've got to know each other better. But it's definitely intimate. I am so captivated by this woman. I'm falling harder for her every day.

Before I know it, we've paid the bill and we're making our way back to the car.

"Oh." Reese says loudly and she clutches her stomach.

Panic hits my chest like icy shards.

"What is it?"

She smiles. "Sorry to scare you, but it made me jump. Here." She grabs my hand and places it on her stomach. "I felt the baby move. It's just flutters at first so you can't feel it, but our baby moved on our first date." She beams. "If that's not the best first date ever, I don't know what is."

I completely agree. "It's perfect."

Back in the house, I grab Reese's hand and lead her straight up to the bedroom. She lifts up her hair so that I can unfasten the zip at the back of her dress, and I lower it before hitching the soft material off her shoulders so it pools at her feet. She stands before me in a plain black bra and cotton panties but she couldn't look any sexier to me if she was in red lace.

I move to my knees and trail my lips and hands over the softly rounded flesh of her stomach.

"Do you have any idea how happy I am right now, Reese?" I kiss her tummy again, and then I put my fingers at the top of her panties and I pull them down. "And now I'm going to make you so happy you scream with joy."

I move her so she's sitting on the edge of the bed and I sit myself between her thighs. I push her legs apart and sit back and look at her spread before me. Her perfect tits are almost bursting out of that black bra and her pink folds are glistening in front of me. I lick up her seam, tasting her essence on my tongue and she groans with pleasure.

"More," she begs.

I place two fingers inside her and push them in and out while my tongue licks and my mouth sucks on her clit. She pushes her pelvis up to meet me, riding my face to get herself off.

She's wild and it's not long before she's spasming over my tongue. I lap up all of her juices and as she starts to come back down, I flip her over the end of the bed and pull her onto her knees. Entering her from behind, we're almost feral as we take what we need from each other. Thrusting in and out I feel my balls tighten and then I'm shooting my load inside her. Placing my fingers on her clit I strum her to a second orgasm and then we collapse together onto the bed.

When we have our breath back, Reese turns to face me.

"Just so you know, I never normally put out on

a first date," she says, trying and failing to keep her face straight.

It's just so amusing, as I look down at her pregnant stomach that I snort and before I know it we're laughing so hard tears stream down our faces.

18

———

REESE

"YOU'RE REALLY HATING this aren't you?" Brandon whispers in my ear while the sonographer takes a few measurements. Thankfully it wasn't the same lady who did our twelve-week scan and watched us bicker like kids the entire time.

"I'm fine. I'm fine," I say in the hope it'll make it true. In reality I'm dying to find out if I'm growing a little girl or boy. My inner control freak is going crazy with her need to know what colour clothes we should be buying and what colour we should be painting the nursery. I know Brandon's only trying to push me out of my comfort zone and that if I couldn't cope he would let me have my way.

He chuckles. "If you really need—"

"No. I want it to be a surprise too. Everything in my life up until you had been planned within an inch of its life. It's time for a change." It pains me to say it, but I'm determined to break the mould. Not that I haven't really by getting myself in this situation in the first place.

"Okay." Brandon squeezes my hand and stares into my eyes. The love I find staring back at me has my eyes burning.

"Everything is looking really good." The sonographer turns the screen and point a few things out on our little bean who is now resembling an actual person. I can make out all its limbs. My eyes lock on the screen and I never want to leave. "That's my baby."

"That's our baby," Brandon echoes sounding equally as emotional. I want to glance over at him and experience the look of awe that I know will be on his face, but I can't drag my eyes away from our little person. It's mind-blowing. That perfect little thing is growing in my belly right now.

"Baby's kicking. Can you feel that, Reese?"

"I can." I barely manage to get the words out through the lump in my throat. "They're saying hello."

"Would you like to know the sex?"

"No, we'd like it to be a surprise." The words are off my tongue before I even have a chance to register my brain telling me that it's the right thing to do.

"Are you sure? You probably won't get another chance to find out now if you regret it."

"I won't regret it. As long as I know he or she is okay in there then I'm all good."

Brandon's soft lips press to my temple but my eyes stay locked on the screen. Another twenty weeks and we'll be able to see what our baby really looks like.

I'm still staring at the scan pictures long after we leave the hospital. "It's just so incredible what our bodies are capable of, don't you think?"

"I know. One drunken fumble and just look what happens."

"Way to ruin the moment." I playfully swat him on the shoulder.

"What? I can say hands down that it was the best thing I've ever done under the influence of alcohol."

"I didn't agree at the time."

"No, maybe not the morning after. I pretty much still hated you then."

"So much so you ran before I even woke up."

Heat colours his cheeks as he thinks back.

"I couldn't bear to have you throw me out. I already felt like a total tool for banging my best mate's little sister, the last thing I needed was a barrel load of abuse from you."

"Probably for the best."

"You're not even going to deny that's what you would have done?"

"Why would I? It's the truth and we both know it. It all worked out in the end though, didn't it, snookums?"

"Sure did, cupcake."

I'm still chuckling at how we found ourselves here when Brandon turns into a retail park.

"What are we doing?"

"I thought today was the perfect day to decorate the nursery. Though I was expecting you to cave about finding out the sex and that we'd need to buy a specific colour."

A zing of excitement races through me. "Can we pick furniture too?" I ask, looking towards the baby store a few shops down from the DIY shop.

"Um... maybe another day. Let's sort the walls first."

I'm disappointed, but still the thought of

making our little one's room look all cute is too appealing to let it fester.

When we leave, Brandon's loaded down with two tubs of paint, an arm full of wallpaper, paste, and all the brushes and tools we could need.

"Don't you already have most of that stuff in your garage?"

"Yeah, but I wanted new for this. It's special."

His excitement is clear in his voice and I can't help but fall that little bit more for him.

Turning, I come to an abrupt stop in front of him. Concern hits his features. "What's wrong?"

"I love you, baby daddy."

Dropping my lips to his, I kiss him in the middle of the car park. Not caring about the cars driving around us trying to find a space or the fact it's drizzling rain. All that matters is this man who's giving me everything.

"I love you too, Reese, but any chance I could go put this down?"

I look down at the stuff hanging from his arms and wince. "Well, if you'd have let me help, you wouldn't be carrying so much."

"Just open the damn boot, woman."

"Sure thing, caveman."

"You're going to need to part with this car

sooner or later you know. We're never going to get a car seat in this thing."

"I know," I say sadly. It's the one thing I've been clinging onto, but I know the time is coming to trade it in for something more sensible.

"We can go this weekend if you like. Any idea what you might want?" I shake my head. I've always had expensive taste when it comes to cars, so I've really no idea what I could get for the money I've got.

<hr>

AS THE SUN begins to set later that day, we're both covered in paint splatters. My back aches and my feet are pounding but the sense of achievement that's swelling my chest is totally worth it.

"It looks incredible, Brandon."

The walls are a soft biscuit colour with one feature wall with paper featuring different colour stars.

"I wish we had the furniture to finish it off," I sulk, now desperate to see our baby's room complete.

"We will soon. Why don't you go and have a bath? You look like you're struggling."

I hate to admit it, but he's right, and the temptation of hot soothing water is a little too much to ignore.

"That sounds like an incredible idea."

"Go and relax. I'll get this all finished off and clean up."

"Thank you for this, Brandon."

"You're more than welcome. Anything for you two." His hand gently brushes over my belly.

There was a time when I never would have believed this was possible. But standing here it's the most natural thing I've ever done. I've had to fight tooth and nail for everything else I've ever done in my life, but this just feels so... right. I thought I'd miss my job and the thrill of winning my client's case, but I really don't. I can honestly say that right now is the happiest I've ever been.

Smiling down at Brandon who's dropped to give my belly a kiss, I thread my fingers into his hair and pull him back up to me. His face is covered in paint thanks to the roller he's been using all afternoon, but he's never looked better.

Reaching forward, I bring our lips together and pepper kisses over his mouth. He allows me a few seconds of control before his hand slides into my hair and his tongue slips past my lips.

"Can't. Get. Enough," he murmurs between kisses.

Pulling back, he rests his forehead against mine. His heaving breath skirts over my face.

"Go... before I take you in our baby's new room."

I almost stay exactly where I am because the offer is so tempting, but my backache makes itself known and I know where I really need to be. There's time for that later.

With one last kiss, I leave him in the room and go to run my bath.

Once I'm settled in the soothing water, I grab my phone and call Sarah.

"So did you find out?"

"Nope, I was strong."

"I can't believe I don't know whether to buy my future godchild blue or pink," she grumbles.

"Godchild? Bit presumptuous, aren't you?"

"After all the years I've had to put up with you? Not at all."

"Hardly. You pissed off up north as soon as you could to get away from me," I say lightheartedly. "So how are things up there?"

"Stressful. The oldest kid is going off the rails. She was suspended from school this afternoon for fighting. I'm at my wits end, and with her parents never here, I really don't know what to do for the best."

"The little shit needs teaching a lesson by the sounds of it."

"I couldn't agree more but there's only so much I can do."

"That sucks. You know, you should just have your own. You can shout at them any time you like then," I say with a laugh, trying to lighten the mood a little.

"Ha, yeah. Chance would be a fine thing. I spend all hours of the day following these little brats around. I don't find much time to go prowling for my own baby daddy."

"Your brother got a best friend?"

"Funny."

We chat for a while longer before she insists I hang up and get out of the bath before I fall asleep in it and drown her godchild.

I can barely put one step in front of the other when I step out of the bathroom a while later wearing one of Brandon's t-shirts that I stole from his drawer.

"I can positively say that that looks better on

you than it does me," he says, climbing the last few stairs.

"I hope you don't mind; my pyjamas are getting a little tight."

"Mind? You look hot as fuck right now. You are more than welcome to wear my clothes any time you like." His eyes drop to my bare feet and slowly make their way up. By the time they hit the hem of his shirt, my thighs are clenching to feel his hands on me.

He steps forward and I wait for his touch and hopefully his kiss, but instead of that, his hand comes over my eyes and he spins me around.

"What are you doing?" I ask in a rush, not liking having my sight removed.

"I've got a surprise for you."

"Oh. I hope it's what's hiding behind those sweatpants."

He chuckles and thrusts his crotch into my arse, making me moan, but when he starts walking me forward and turns, it's not into our room.

"You ready?"

"You naked?"

"You're insatiable."

"It's the baby. Are you complaining?"

"Not at all. Just worried it'll dry up afterwards."

"I don't think we're going to have a problem. You've seen yourself in a mirror, right?"

"So you only want me for my body?"

"Yep. There isn't all that much else that's worth it, slob."

"I could say the same, Ice Queen."

His hand that's not around my eyes, skims up my hip and under his t-shirt so he can place his fingers over my belly.

Leaning into my ear, his breath tickles, making goosebumps prick my skin. "One. Two. Three." He removes his hand and I blink a couple of times to make my eyes focus.

"Brandon," I breathe, not able to find the words for what I'm looking at. "Oh my god, did you make all this?"

"I did."

"It's... it's incredible." I look between the hand-crafted furniture that now fills our baby's room through tear-filled eyes. "This must have taken you hours."

"I've been working on it all for months."

"Wow," I breathe. Walking over, I run my fingertips over the cot before opening the chest of drawers with a changing table sitting on the top and a perfectly sized wardrobe for little clothes.

"Do you like it?" There's a slight wobble to his voice like he's unsure.

"Brandon, it's so beautiful. I'm lost for words."

His arms wrap around me as I stare down into the cot, trying to imagine what it'll look like with our baby wiggling around inside it.

"I'm so sorry I ever called you a lazy, talentless slob."

"I'm sorry I ever made you think I was one. I was just lost, Reese. But you rescued me. You found the man I'd hidden beneath heartache and hair and you've made him better than he ever was before."

A sob bubbles up my throat and I'm turning into his arms. He kisses the top of my head and expresses once again how much he loves me. I've no idea how I ended up here, but I never want to leave.

August

MY LIFE IS PERFECT.

Our life is perfect.

And in approximately a month's time our life will be even more perfect.

Today the sun is shining and so we're taking a walk in the park before we nip to the shops to stock up on nappies and other items that are going to become essentials in the upcoming weeks.

Reese is blooming. As the sun shines on her I'm glad it's not overbearingly hot. Her pale blue strappy summer dress floats down, and the gentle breeze blows it against her bump, now very prominent. Her skin is tanned and golden. She looks the picture of health and she has the slightest little waddle to her walk.

"Can you believe that soon we'll be doing this pushing a pram around with our baby in it?" Reese smiles up at me.

"It doesn't seem real, but I can't wait to meet our baby. I wonder what it'll look like?"

"Maybe a little boy who looks just like his daddy?"

"Or a little girl who looks just like her mummy?"

We're corny and cheesy and I absolutely don't give a fuck.

Because we're in love.

And I've decided that as soon as that baby is here and we're a little more settled, I'm going to propose to Reese.

Because this woman has shown me to not be afraid to love, and I realise that what I thought I had with Naomi was nothing. That was first love, with its crushing disappointments while the body and brain learn about relationships. What I have with Reese is real, warts and all, 'I'd die for you' kind of love. She's my world.

The Ice Queen and the Slob. There's a new one for Disney.

WE MOVE onto the shops buying cute little outfits we don't need because the baby's neutral wardrobe is already vast, and another cuddly toy that just might be the one the baby loves hard.

Finally, I can see Reese is tiring. "Let's just nip quickly to the supermarket. Tell me what you want this evening for dinner and then you can put your feet up while I cook."

"Sounds good to me."

I tell Reese she can stay in the car, but she insists on coming in with me. "Can we get some more nappies?" she asks.

I begin laughing. "Reese, how many packs of nappies do we need to have in? The supermarket is five minutes away from home."

She gives me a pout that I currently can't resist. "Oh come on then. One more pack won't hurt."

We're in the nappy aisle when we hear a voice.

"Hello, bitch." A sour-faced, thin, tall man comes up to Reese, invading her personal space.

She jumps. I step in between the man and her, my muscles tensing ready to kill him if I need to.

"Got a problem, friend?"

"I'm no friend. Just it's a little bit rich, seeing the lawyer who took my kids away from me, buying nappies ready for her own kid coming," he shouts over my shoulder. "I hope some fucker takes yours away from you, so you know what it's like."

He stamps off and I look around. "I need to get a security guard."

Reese grasps my shoulder; she's trembling. "No, let's just leave all this and get home, please? I just want to go home."

"Are you sure you're okay? Do you need to sit down?"

Reese takes some deep breaths. "I'm okay. In fact, give me a minute and then let's pay for this shopping. I refuse to be intimidated by that bastard. And he wonders why he lost access to his kids."

We take our time and eventually leave the store and make our way to our car. What happens next is so unexpected that it takes a moment for me to process it's really happened.

A car screeches through the spaces next to us and hits Reese. I watch in what feels like slow motion as she goes sprawling over its bonnet landing on the floor. I run to her but she's out cold.

"Reese. Reese. Wake up, please," I plead looking around me for help.

People come running; one tells me she's a first aider, someone else calls an ambulance. The first aider takes over checking Reese is breathing while I turn to the man who has exited his car.

"He did it. He threatened her and ran her over. Get the police," I shout.

The man starts to protest. "I just wanted to scare her. That's all. I didn't mean to hit her. My foot slipped on the accelerator."

I'm not interested in anything he has to say. All my thoughts are with my girlfriend and baby. It seems forever before the sirens of the ambulance arrive and we're taken to hospital.

Reese begins to stir as she's lifted into the ambulance. "What...?"

"Reese? My name is Moira and I'm a paramedic. We're taking you to hospital, sweetheart. You were knocked down. Just keep still for us while we check you over."

"M- my baby?" Reese's voice breaks as she asks.

"We need to get you to hospital and checked over. Let us do our job and you just try to relax.

Your husband's here." She nods to me to move closer. "He'll hold your hand while we get there, okay?"

And that's what I do. I hold her hand all the way to hospital, stroking her thumb and telling her everything will be okay when the truth is I have no idea. I'm not and have never been a religious man but in my head I pray to every deity there is.

We arrive at Accident and Emergency. The obstetric department is only around the corner and I don't know who we need. I feel so helpless. Reese is whizzed through with staff shouting out words I don't know the meaning of and I'm asked to wait in a waiting room.

I'm left alone and my girlfriend and unborn baby are gone and at the mercy of doctors and fate.

I fall to a seat, place my head in my hands, and take a moment to just try to gather my breath. Then I pick up my phone and call Jack.

HE ARRIVES WITH RHIAN, and his mother and his father. I look from one to the other of them knowing they do not have a good history. Reese's mum touches my arm. "She's our daughter. We'll be civil. What is happening?" I look to her father and he nods his head.

"I don't know. She was taken through to the main hospital and no one has been out yet."

Reese's mum goes to make enquiries and before long a doctor comes out of the main doors asking for her. We step forward.

After finding out who we are he begins to speak.

"Reese has a concussion. Other than that her vital signs are stable. She's been very lucky. However, the shock of the impact has triggered early labour. She's been moved over to the labour ward." He looks at me. "If you'd like to make your way there, your baby is on the way."

"But everything is okay?" I ask.

"Reese is okay, apart from needing to be watched for a concussion. The baby is being monitored and so far everything is stable."

"Oh thank God." Tears fill my eyes and I turn around to the others to find every one of us is sobbing.

"We'll go find a coffee shop or something. Keep us informed." Rhian says, coming over and hugging me. "Now go!"

Adrenaline fires me up and I run all the way.

Pushing through the doors, I find Reese laid down on a bed with monitors on her stomach.

"Brandon. Thank God."

"Is everything okay?"

The midwife nods. "Everything is progressing smoothly so far. We're likely to be a while with it being mum's first labour. However this little monkey has decided to come a month early and so we'll be monitoring things closely. Plus, we also have to keep an extra eye on mummy here, seeing as she has that nasty bruise on her forehead.

It's true. Reese's forehead has a large yellowish bruise appearing and is swollen. I pull up a seat at the side of her.

"What happened to Mr Harper?"

I shake my head. "I don't know and we'll deal with him when you're both home safe. The police will have him in custody by now. Right now, we're concentrating on a healthy baby and a healthy mama, okay?"

"Okay," she says, and then she squeezes my hand hard as another contraction hits.

ELEVEN HOURS LATER, Breanna Rose is born weighing 5lb 8oz. She's tiny but perfect, with a small smattering of fair hair and a rosebud mouth. My heart is full and bursting with love for both her and for her mother. I have never been so happy in my entire life.

While they clean up mum and baby, I go outside and phone Jack to tell him he's become an uncle. He and his parents had left once they'd known the birth would take hours.

"Congrats, man. You sure they're both okay?" Jack asks.

"They're perfect but staying in a day or so for observations." As I put my phone down it rings again and it's the police telling me that the Harper guy had been drinking and had been arrested for several offences. I explain that Reese has had the baby and I'm offered congratulations along with assurances that he'll be prosecuted.

In another life I would want to rip his head off and stuff it up his arsehole, but there's no room in my mind for that lowlife. Not now I'm reassured that my baby mama and baby are safe.

I make my way back to the room that holds my world.

One week later

THE AWESOME SOUNDS of laughter and chatter fill the air of our home. Reese is in the living room, talking away to her childhood friend Sarah who has come down from the Lake District. So much for my having tidied up my act and Reese having got rid of her clothes and shoes; the house is filled to the brim with gifts for the baby and the new parents, along with opened packets of nappies, bibs, and all the other paraphernalia that goes with having babies.

I wouldn't have it any other way.

I watch from the doorway as Sarah coos over the bundle in her arms and Reese watches over protectively.

I wink at Sarah as she looks over at me and she nods.

"Reese, honey. Sarah's got Bree there safely. Can I borrow you to come check on this box I found in the nursery?"

Reese's brow crumples with consideration. "What does it look like?"

"It's hard to describe. It's easier to show you."

She rolls her eyes at Sarah. "Men," she exclaims. "I'm glad I've had a girl."

I fold my arms as I look at her. "And who's to say we've finished? Maybe next time it'll be a boy."

"I just gave birth a week ago. If you value your testicles, you'll shut up right now." She stands up. "Let's go see what this goddamn box is."

"Ooh is it getting a tad chilly in here, almost *icy?*" I mock, receiving side-eye from Reese as she moves past me.

I follow her up the stairs to the nursery.

"It's in the cot," I tell her.

She walks over and then turns around to look at me.

"What are you up to, Brandon Weston?"

I smile and walk over to the cot where I pick up the hand-carved wooden box that has Reese's name engraved on it.

Then I drop to one knee and open the box.

Inside, the lid is hand-carved with the words 'Will you marry me?' and the bottom of the box has a diamond solitaire resting on silk.

"Reese Connors. You have brought the most precious jewel into my life. Our daughter. It's only fair you get a precious jewel in return. I love you. Will you marry me?"

"Y- yes. Yes, I will. Oh my god, yes. When I've lost the baby weight though, okay?"

"You are perfect, Reese, just as you are. Perfect... for me."

I place the ring on her finger. It's a little snug, but then she just gave birth and I had to go on the sizes of old rings. It's all fixable and hell, I'd buy her another in a heartbeat. She moves her hand this way and that, beaming. I sweep her into my arms and lower my mouth to hers, crushing her in a passionate kiss.

When I let go, she's fidgeting. "You're dying to tell Sarah, aren't you?" I laugh.

"Yup." She giggles. "Was she in on it?"

"Of course."

She sets off downstairs, "Sarah! I'm engaged," she squeals.

I turn back around looking at the nursery and then I head in the direction of the shrieks coming from the living room and I think how much my life has changed since Jack and Aiden staged my intervention.

I wouldn't change a thing.

EPILOGUE

Reese

WITH MY BABY in my arms and my man by my side, I walk into the private room at InHale where we're celebrating our engagement.

I wasn't all that bothered about being the centre of attention and having a party, but Brandon insisted that he wanted to show both me and Bree off. I couldn't really argue with that.

He stands aside and allows me to enter first and I find everyone I love staring back at me.

My mum comes rushing over first so she can get her hands on her granddaughter. Bree is whipped out of my arms and I watch as Mum coos at her.

I always thought women who claimed being a mother was a fulfilling job were talking crap. I thought I needed the pressure and the stress of a courtroom to feel fulfilled, but shit, was I wrong. Looking after my daughter is by far the best and most gratifying thing I've ever done in my life. The love that pours from her little eyes every time she stares up at me fills me with such joy. She might only be two months old but already I can't recall what my life was like without her. And Brandon for that matter.

Maybe one day I'll return to work, but I don't intend to return to law, not after I nearly lost my baby. Clive sent some flowers around when Bree was born, along with an apology: a note saying Rich had had to be sacked for making a pass at Chantelle and they hoped I'd consider them if I ever worked in family law again. I sawed the whole lot up using Brandon's power saw.

I make my way around the room, greeting everyone and accepting their congratulations. More than a few of them delight in telling me that they never thought they'd see the day I settled down. I must admit, I was one of them. But the life

I never expected has turned out to be a million times better than the perfect one I thought I had.

I just turn to say hello to Scott who's serving us tonight when someone walks through the door that I wasn't expecting to see.

"Sarah!" I squeal, rushing over to wrap my arms around her shoulders. She told me she wasn't going to make it because of work. She was lucky to get away to come and see Bree after she was born so she thought asking to come back for a party was pushing it. "You're here." Tears sting my eyes that she's done whatever she has to be here to celebrate with me tonight. I never admitted, or even really accepted, how much I missed her when she moved away. But since Brandon has thawed my cold heart, I tell her how much I miss her every time I talk to her.

It's not until I pull back that I see she's not fully looking me in the eye and I note she has tears welling.

"What's wrong?"

"Nothing. I'm just happy for you. This is your night and I'm so happy that you got your man and your baby. Now let's get on with celebrating. I put your engagement gift on the table over there, but I have something for Bree. Where is she?"

"Don't bullshit me. I know you. What's wrong?"

"Okay, fine. But please don't make a big deal about it. We'll talk about it properly once tonight is over." I nod at her, desperate to know what has tears pooling in her eye. "I lost my job."

"Oh fuck. I'm so sorry why?"

"A misunderstanding."

I narrow my eyes at her, but she just shakes her head. Following her wishes not to talk about it, I link my arm with hers and drag her into the room.

We're halfway to the bar when she freezes.

"What's wrong?" I ask when I turn to her and see all the blood drain from her face.

"It's n- nothing." I don't believe it for a second and my doubts are confirmed when I hear a familiar voice.

"Sarah?" Scott asks, his brows drawn together before his eyes drop to take her in.

"Christ, could my life get any worse?" she mutters. "I need a drink. Now."

Her arm tightens in mine and she drags me towards the bar and away from Scott without saying a single word to him.

"Don't," she warns when I open my mouth to

ask. "Add it to the list of things to ask me about tomorrow."

Sarah manages to turn the conversation towards Bree knowing that it's probably the only thing that will distract me from asking the many questions that are currently filling my head.

"Can I borrow my girl?" Brandon asks, coming to stand behind me and wrapping his hands around my waist.

"Of course."

Pressing his lips to my ear, I can't help my eyes fluttering closed. "Dance with me?"

"I thought you'd never ask."

He takes my hand and leads me to our makeshift dance floor. He pulls me tight up against his body. His hard lines press against what's left of my baby weight. I thought it would bother me, but with Brandon both telling and showing me daily how much loves me and my body, it's not bothered me one bit. Plus, it's the result of our gorgeous daughter who's now in the arms of Brandon's mum. I'll carry around a few extra pounds for the rest of my life for her.

"The next time we do this you'll be my wife. Who'd have imagined the Ice Queen and the Slob having a happy ever after?"

A wide smile spreads across my face at the thought.

"I can't wait, snookums."

219

Ready to discover why Sarah's lost her job? Grab her forbidden, daddy's best friend romance, **SINGLE DADDY SEDUCTION NOW.**
Read on for a sneak peek!

CHAPTER ONE - SARAH

"She hit me, Daddy. She hit me."

"No, I didn't." I protested looking at Jim's face. "Why on earth would I do that? I've looked after Melinda, Jessica, and Lana for three years, surely you're not going to believe her." But I looked at his face and knew he did. "Look, just give it an hour and I'll sit in my room and then ask her again. She'll change her mind and then she can apologise and..."

"I've called the police."

My jaw dropped. "You've done what?"

"My daughter says you hit her earlier. On the

back and on the leg. I asked if you'd hit her before and she said yes."

I looked at Melinda. Nine years old, she'd always been a nightmare to look after. Demanding, argumentative. Lots of, 'You're not my mum'. No, Mummy was too busy running a magazine to be at home and if this is what her version of parenthood was like I couldn't blame her. But I thought we'd been getting somewhere. I mean it had been three years for goodness' sake. But now, for whatever reason, Melinda had told a lie that I wasn't sure we could ever get back from.

My face paled as the thought came, what if the police believed her?

"Please wait in your room until the police arrive. Be packing your bags and then once they've left, I'd like you to leave. I won't of course be paying you for this last month."

The way Jim looked at me was soul destroying. He and Kelly had been so grateful they'd said for my patience with their children and for my not leaving them when other nanny positions became available. Good nannies were hard to find and so we could basically choose our own wages and perks.

As I sighed and made my way up to my room, I walked past Melinda who gave me a satisfied smirk.

I was sure she wouldn't be looking that happy when mummy and daddy found out the truth. God, I hoped they did.

"Would you like a coffee, Madam?" I look up at the woman dressed in her rail uniform. I'd splashed out even though I was minus my latest wage and upgraded to first class for the journey back to my parents' house in Twickenham from Crewe. Hellishly, my journey from Oxenholme to Crewe was spent sat near a screaming kid and I'd had my fill of children for now.

I accepted a coffee but said no to a muffin. The thoughts of what had happened yesterday afternoon were still at the front of my mind. I just kept ruminating. Seeing the situation again and again and again. The police had been and said there was no evidence, but in the circumstances they understood the parents' concerns and investigations would be ongoing. I wasn't sure what they meant but would look into my own legal action from home. My phone had beeped incessantly since as the local nannies got the goss and tried to find out the truth. None had been my friends. Everyone in the nanny world was a competitor, friendly until they wanted your job and then they'd try to swoop in.

After spending the night in a budget hotel and not getting much sleep, first thing this morning I checked out and got on a train home. My parents didn't know I was coming. The last thing I needed was my mum wittering down the phone last night. I'd needed time to think things over. The situation seemed better explained face to face. Thank goodness I still had my room at their house; a base where I could decide what I did next. Fact is, I had fuck all chance of a nanny job, or maybe any job, while 'investigations continued' and the little savings I had amassed wouldn't last long.

What the fuck was I going to do? All because of a spoilt, lying brat. I was done with kids. Done. Did not want to spend my time with anymore brats anytime soon.

Almost home, I catch a cab from the station down to my parents semi-detached on Lincoln Avenue. As it pulls up outside the driveway and I see the familiar porch, a huge sigh of relief floods through me. I'm home. My parents will know what to do and they'll welcome me in their loving arms. They never wanted me to go there in the first place; my mum felt it was too far away. I'll spend some time letting them spoil me and then hopefully the recent incident will blow over and I can start afresh.

I ring the doorbell, but no one answers. Shouting comes from inside the house and my brow furrows. Then I hear an ear-piercing shriek.

"Can someone get the goddamn door while I put the dishes away and get a wash on, or am I the only one around here capable of doing anything?" I hear my mum shout. My mum never shouts. What on earth is going on?

Finally, I hear footsteps. "If this is a Jehovah's Witness or some charity collector, I'm going to give them a right earbashing." I hear my younger brother say.

What's Luke doing here?

The door opens and my brother peers at my face.

"Haven't you got a key?" He turns towards the house before he hears my answer, that my mother took it because she lost their spare and has never replaced it.

"It's Sarah." He yells.

There's another scream and my two-year-old

niece Marley comes belting through, not a stitch of clothing on.

"Auntie Say-yah." She flings herself at my legs and the chocolate mousse she had around her mouth transfers straight to my skinny jeans. Fabulous.

"What are you doing here?" Luke asks me.

"Can I actually get through the door, or are you keeping me outside all day?"

He steps back so I can finally walk inside, picking up Marley who wails at being separated from my leg.

I drag my cases inside, rolling my eyes at him picking up his kid instead of my cases. Then again, did I really want coating in more chocolate mousse? It hasn't escaped my notice that my wishes to be child free have immediately been thwarted, but a visit from my brother and niece is nice. I don't get to see them much.

"Where's Liv?" I ask as I walk into the living room, looking around for my brother's partner. They've been together since they met at school at sixteen. Marley came along when they were twenty. Liv calls their relationship passionate. I call it being at loggerheads a lot.

"She's in bed. She's feeling sick."

"Oh poor thing. So you got here and she was taken ill? Does she need a doctor?"

My mum walks in, drying her hands on a dishcloth. Dad bought her a dishwasher, but she refuses to use it, says it doesn't clean properly.

"Sarah! Why didn't you tell me you were visiting?"

"Well, that's the thing. Is Dad here?"

"He's at work, darling. Which is where I thought you'd be."

"Yes, well, I've had to take some time off, so I've come home. I'll be back a while. If it's okay, I'll just go run upstairs with my things."

"You can't." My brother tells me. "I've already told you. Liv's in bed."

"She's in my bed?" I'm aghast.

"No, she's in our bed. That's where we've been staying for the last three weeks since we got evicted."

"Come again?" I state. I can see our mother look from one of us to the other and she steps forward, just as she always did when we were about to take a chunk out of each other as kids.

"Luke and Olivia are staying here with Marley for a while. Marley's in Luke's old room, and Luke and Olivia are in your room."

I turn to Luke. "Why did you get evicted? It was for arguing wasn't it?"

He looks at the floor confirming everything.

"I don't know why you stay together with all the rowing you do."

"It's just banter. Nothing serious. It's just Liv likes to throw things and she threw a mug and it hit the kitchen window."

I stand up straight and move into his personal space. "Well, you're all going to have to pack yourself into your old room because I'm back."

"I'm not moving Liv. She's got to be looked after in her condition."

Please God no.

"What condition?"

"She's six weeks pregnant."

I breathe audibly through my nose. "Why has no one told me any of this? That you've been evicted and that Liv's preggers again? That you're staying at our parents' house?"

I look accusingly at my mother.

She just shrugs her shoulders. "We didn't want to worry you while you were so far away, so we just figured we'd catch you up on things when you next came for a visit, and here you are and now you're all caught up."

Is my family for real?

"So I can't stay here then? In my own room. Because my brother has two rooms."

"Of course you can stay. Don't be silly, Sarah. We have a perfectly good sofa. You can sleep in the living room for now. How long were you thinking of staying?"

Well it had been for a while.

"I don't know. How long are you staying?" I ask my brother. "Is there a chance I'll get my room back anytime soon?"

"We're not looking for anywhere until Liv starts feeling better."

I stamp my feet. Twenty-five and stamping my feet like Marley.

Talking of Marley...

"Where's your daughter?" I ask Luke.

He looks around. "Oh shit, and she still has the chocolate mousse."

"Marley?" He shouts running into the hallway.

Me and mum follow him out and find Marley in the downstairs toilet smearing the remainder of her chocolate mousse all over the walls and floor. It looks like shit is coated everywhere but luckily it smells far nicer.

"How has it spread so far?" Luke wails.

"Did she actually eat any of it?" I laugh.

"It's okay for you laughing. You don't have to clean it all up do you?"

"I'll get a cloth." My mum says.

"You'll not clean it up either." I hiss at Luke. "You'll get Mum to do it. You've always been lazy. It wouldn't surprise me if you got evicted on purpose while Liv's out of action so you can get Mum and Dad doing everything for you."

"Get lost. Why aren't you at your hoity-toity job anyway? Slumming it back here, aren't you?"

Something in my expression must give the game away.

A slow smile builds on his face. "Have you lost your job?"

"Sssh."

"Oh wow, the golden girl isn't so golden after all."

My mum comes through with a wet cloth. "Everyone out so I can deal with this."

"Luke should be doing it." I protest.

He picks up Marley. "I have this one to clean up."

"You should clean the toilet walls first."

"It's fine, Sarah." My mum says. "It's just

chocolate mousse. If it was another brown substance, I'd leave Luke to it."

Luke smiles at me victorious until Marley lets out a fart and follows through.

"Oh dear. I'd better leave you to it." I smirk back. "Thought I was the one having a shitty time of it, but it looks like I'm not alone."

GRAB SINGLE DADDY SEDUCTION NOW

ABOUT TRACY LORRAINE

Tracy Lorraine is new adult and contemporary romance author. Tracy is in her thirties and lives in a cute Cotswold village in England with her husband and daughter. Having always been a bookaholic with her head stuck in her Kindle, Tracy decided to try her hand at a story idea she dreamt up and hasn't looked back since.

Be the first to find out about new releases and offers. Sign up to my newsletter here.

If you want to know what I'm up to and see teasers and snippets of what I'm working on, then you need to be in my Facebook group. Join Tracy's Angels here.

Keep up to date with Tracy's books at

www.tracylorraine.com

9 798799 711702